The Last Confession

by the Author

Morris West

The Last Confession

FOREWARD BY

Thomas Keneally

The Toby Press

First American Edition 2003

The Toby Press *LLC*
www.tobypress.com

ISBN 1 902881 44 3, *paperback original*

A CIP catalogue record for this title
is available from the British Library

Typeset in Garamond by Jerusalem Typesetting

Printed and bound in the United States by
Thomson-Shore Inc., Michigan

I wish to thank with all my heart Thomas Keneally for his generous and wonderful Foreword, Angelo Loukakis for his Editor's Note and Beryl Barraclough for her contribution to the Epilogue and help in many other ways. All of them together have made publication of this book possible.

Joy West

Tom Keneally

Foreword

When I first went to London in 1970, as a young writer from the ends of the earth making the prescriptive visit to the then-centre of the literary world, I found there was an Australian there before me. His name, Morris West, was in large letters in the West End, outside the theatre where his play *The Heretic* was being performed. Having known from his earlier books that he was concerned with the anomalies of faith, with the question of where, within the legalisms of the Church, there was a place for transcendence, joy, exuberance of thought, I was not surprised to hear that the play concerned that most exuberant of all Italian heretics, Giordano Bruno.

Bruno was that perilous thing, a free spirit, and suffered death for his right to certain concepts. I knew from conversations with Morris later in his life, in the frank and jovial light of Avalon, New South Wales, that Giordano Bruno was a soul mate, someone with whose life history Morris identified, even though Morris possessed a somewhat less strident temperament than Bruno's. "Failed priest," as Morris has Bruno declare in this tale, "fugitive monk, magus with a box of conjuring tricks, boaster, prevaricator, would-be torchbearer trudging through his own darkness, garrulous in dialogue, viperous in debate." Like Morris though, Bruno was a prolific writer on a range of subjects, and an author of plays. More importantly, he finds himself crying, when accused of having gone to Zurich to become a Calvinist: "I was a troubled soul, trying to find a hat to fit his bursting brainbox." Morris too spent his life nobly in a search for such a hat.

I know it is a matter of consolation to Morris's family that he went as writers always say they want to go, at his desk and at the end of a particularly good paragraph. By contrast, his friend across the centuries, Bruno, died at the end of seven years of interrogation, harsh penal treatment, and occasional torture, in an horrific display of institutional—in this case, Inquisitorial—vengefulness. Morris piquantly summarises the man's very human dilemma, the contrast between the huge, striding reach of intellect and the limits of the body. "You wrote so confidently of an infinite universe and a plural world beyond our view, yet you cannot control even this tiny rat-hole on your own planet." Morris also strode the universe, but in the end fell, as we all do if we die peacefully, to some intimate and minute betrayal by his own body. Death came for Bruno long ago, on a pyre in the Campo dei Fiori in Rome on 17 February 1600. Yet, as you will see, Morris's last paragraph, written in the last seconds of his life, connects himself and the long-dead heretic, and is prophetic both for Bruno—for a writer can surely be a prophet, a sayer of truth, backwards in time—as for Morris himself, and for the rest of us still left in the human dilemma.

This is a book suffused by the expectation of death and the necessity of love as the sole viable riposte to it. It is not a secret to Morris's friends and readers that he was a man of the broadest compassion. His love of humanity was combined with a confident worldliness and a sharp awareness of the temptations which orthodoxy held out to those of authoritarian, absolutist bent. He knew that passion for the strictest orthodoxy was a besetting human problem, applying equally to the ideologues of the Inquisition as to the devotees of certain modern economic and political theories. These modern manifestations have, like the strictures of the Inquisition, little time for the individual as more than an obeyer, a pliable voter, a passive consumer of what is on offer. Like Giordano, Morris could not understand why, to bring a man to the mercy of God, the authorities had first to destroy him. Like Giordano, Morris would have liked to see the Church influenced by broader philosophies than a tradition of narrow legalism more likely to cherish authority rather than love. Like Giordano too, Morris saw this narrowness as deriving unimaginatively from the highly structured and rigorous theology of St Thomas Aquinas, which was based on the philosophic method of the Greek philosopher Aristotle. And like Giordano, Morris cherished equally, or perhaps better, that challenging sense of unutterable mysteries some scholars found in Plato and tried to bring to Catholicism.

This fight between the upholders of Plato and those of Aristotle is an ancient contest in the Church. It was dramatised in Umberto Eco's *The Name of the Rose,* in which the hero monk-detective of the tale argues, in a grand set-piece debate, for the Platonist tradition which might leave souls free of the strictness of that same Inquisition which ended Bruno's life.

Giordano, the disgraced monk, died for challenging the legalistic approach to faith and for trying to see what light the Protestant reformers threw on traditional dogma. His huge intellectual playfulness, which we see in Morris's narrative as extending not only to such questions as the Virgin Birth, the celibacy of clerics, the existence of parallel worlds, but also to conjuring and tricks of memory, was willing to take in, examine and write volumes on the entire spectrum of assertions, whether they came from the Vatican, Luther or Calvin. Bruno was trying to assess and fit into a pattern the ideas of a world altering massively under the influence of the Reformation; a world which Copernicus had now shown to be a mere outer fragment of a near-infinite universe. Morris spent his life in that same spirit. To get to truth he was willing to examine all ideas, even if they lay beyond that fortress of those ironbound dogmas which some people consider the essence of faith, the measure of the human soul, and the solitary. path to redemption. He spent his lifetime, in his journeyings and in his books, the way a human should: as a pilgrim. Bruno ran up against a Church which had lost millions of its members to the whirlwind Reformation, and was thus not in an expansive mood. Morris spent his last years in a Church which was also digging in against independence of conscience, modernity, secularism, and post-industrial reality. Both of them struggled heroically with what they loved.

There are a few things I want to say about Morris—now that death has put an end to his exceptional career—which might not have been adequately covered in his obituaries. First of all, he was a working class lad, unused to privilege, unhelped by any inheritance. His background made him appreciative of what a privilege it was to be a writer, to have a readership across the world, to be a voice. He did honour to his craft and talent and great fame by being a highly professional writer. I always said this about him publicly, and some people looked askance at the word 'professional', as if it were a less than flattering description. To me, it's one of the best things you can say about any writer, for survival—and the capacity to reach people—depends on it. He treated his career as something worthy of serious care, serious application and devotion, and serious organisation. And as a mark of that seriousness, it should always be remembered by Australian writers that Morris, through his energy and his financial input, was one of the small band of creators of the Australian Society of Authors. This society still gives advice and help to writers in their relationship with the government, publishers and the readers of the Commonwealth. It devised a minimum contract which is now observed by all reputable publishers. It achieved Public Lending Right (compensation for writers whose works were held in public libraries), put in place a system of photocopying copyright compensation, campaigned for Educational Lending Right, and gave the craft of writing a high profile in Australian society.

Morris also informally supplied economic assistance to a number of writers, and I feel that that generosity has never been adequately noted, nor would he have wanted it to be noted. But it is time to do so.

Morris showed the way to other Australians too. It is difficult to remember that forty years ago, Australian writers were rare and neglected fauna indeed, occupants of a forgotten continent and, in many cases, afflicted with a sense of inferiority hard to recapture in these days of greater cultural confidence. Morris was one of that small group who normalised the proposition that Australians could be published and read not only by their fellow citizens but by the world. This was a cultural service whose impact cannot be overstated.

After his return to Australia and to beautiful Pittwater, where he lived with Joy amidst splendid paintings on a splendid shore, Morris became an elder of our community. He was a questing and sane voice for Australian Catholics who were trying to balance their individual good sense and conscience against the often absolutist magisterium of the Church. But he also commented frequently, in *The Australian* and elsewhere, on our struggle for a civil society, and on political and administrative arrogance. Morris was an elder of our tribe, with an urgent and humane voice. For that as well he will be missed, and it is one more reason I consider it an honour to introduce to you the last of his words, the most essential of his tales.

Angelo Loukakis

Editor's Note

I t was my privilege to work with Morris West as his editor and publisher between 1993 and 1999. When Morris first proposed to take as his subject for this, his final and unfinished novel, the life of Giordano Bruno, he called to tell me as much in a mood of excitement and relief. Relief because through the latter part of 1998 and early 1999 he had in mind a novel of an entirely different kind—a contemporary and largely psychological/moral portrait of a type of character he knew well, someone whom he had described in shorthand to me as a 'money-man'. In the end, he was glad to abandon the project as it had failed to engage his interest enough to energise any writing.

Having freed himself from something which we both felt was going to have to be 'forced' into existence rather than find its way more smoothly onto the page, Morris was now keenly excited by the alternative, by the prospect of a novel on an historical figure who held for him not only great intellectual interest but considerable personal meaning. There were various motives pushing him towards a work on the figure of Bruno. Morris had felt through much of his adult life a deep connection with the story of the Italian heretic's life and death. As early as 1969 he had written a play on this complex, disputative, and in some ways indistinct figure; in retrospect it seems natural that he would eventually turn his novelist's talent to a narrative work. There was another consideration: he was very aware that the time left to him for further writing was limited, given his increasingly fragile health. He was determined, then, that his last novel be one that seriously mattered and one which perhaps might even become the crowning achievement.

It is worth going deeper into the sources of Morris's interest in a Dominican monk and wandering scholar four hundred years dead. Listening to him speak with such animation in what was then his eighty-second year, it was clear that there was something more than a writer's attraction to a great story with potential for fiction. He was moved by—more, had felt his life had been intimately touched by—the man whom he described in *A View from the Ridge*[1] as "like all of us, a contradictory character—a muddled philosopher, an arrogant scholar, a boaster in his cups, a poet in his quiet hours, scared, venal, compromising—and yet, in sum, a figure of heroic proportions".

To anyone unfamiliar with Morris West's own life and career, the choice of subject for this last novel may seem arcane or eccentric. Yet the connections are many and clear: Bruno was an apostate, an enquirer prone to questioning orthodoxy, keen to lecture and teach others, a traveller and intellectual quester. Morris, in his own life, had on more than one occasion found himself uneasy with the teachings of the church into which he had been baptised and which claimed his allegiance. He, like Bruno, had at first attempted to do honour to that church as a religious and to proclaim the teachings of Christ. Bruno nominally remained within his order, eventually to be burned at the stake as a heretic. Morris's time within the formal church brought him to no such mortal crisis of course; after seven years with the Christian Brothers, he was able—in the midst, never-

1 *A View from the Ridge*, Morris West, HarperCollins *Publishers*, 1996; a chronicle of Morris West's life and beliefs.

theless, of much personal difficulty and soul searching—to withdraw before taking final vows. But Morris West was ever conscious of the tendencies in his church to oppress through doctrine and dogma; it was something he fought against all his life and is one of the major themes of *The Last Confession*.

So how to tell the life of one who was famously at odds with the same loveless and prohibitive philosophies all those centuries ago, and who in the end died for it? Morris's method was to attempt what he termed a 'reconstructive' portrait. He chose to present a series of recollections and commentary in the form of a 'diary', purportedly written by Bruno during the passage of 'real time' over the last weeks of his imprisonment and leading up to his execution (that is, between 21 December 1599 and 17 February 1600). He knew that in doing so, a proper degree of narrative momentum would be generated; but just as importantly, along the way one would get the creation of a character *by* that character.

Morris was many things as a writer but above all he was a master of the rhetoric of fiction. He knew that his job was to convince and persuade. He knew the importance of persuading readers to a point of view, and he knew just how to do it—this was fundamental to the kind of writer he was. Morris West was one of the world's finest exponents of what might be termed the 'moral thriller', the novel which assays questions of honour and conscience through the testing of individual character in circumstances not always of the individual's making. In Bruno, he was drawn to a man who held fast to the freedom of his thought against the pernicious force of those who used dogma and doctrine to deny life, in all senses.

As he set to work on this new novel, and we spoke from time to time, one particular encounter stays with me. Some instance of social oppression was in the news at the time, and Morris was especially incensed; here was a first class example of the regimentation of human thought, of the pernicious mechanisms used to bring such ends about, and of our very liberty to think at all. These, he said, were precisely the things he wished to highlight through a retelling of the life and death of Giordano Bruno. Bruno's drama, he argued, was utterly contemporaneous with our own; he was passionately convinced it could be retold for a modern audience. And if there was one central point to be got across, it was this: in certain times and circumstances, to be true to yourself may require you to pay the highest price.

The Last Confession was not intended to be a 'light' book; equally, it was both easy and hard for Morris West to write. While the writing process made its own demands on his physical resources, there were few problems at the level of narrative technique—the prose left to us is characteristically fluid (although not as finely worked or as finished as it would inevitably have been after a second pass), the imagery vivid, all the experience and skill of his art and craft is plentifully evident. Though it is unfinished, there is enough here to allow the reader to see the important themes of West's work surfacing one final time.

The novel has not been 'edited' in the conventional sense. This has been a deliberate decision, in as much as it can hardly be proper to rework or cut sections of prose without authorial involvement. Like other and earlier editors of his, I found Morris a determined advocate of his own work during the editorial process, a man not always amenable to suggestions for improving the text, but one prepared to be convinced if you had a good argument. I regret that we were never able to get down to that activity with *The Last Confession*, as much as I was looking forward to the 'sport' of it.

For me, there remains the satisfaction of recalling Morris speak passionately on the novel's progress, of listening to him read a section out aloud from time to time, either over the phone or in person (he was a fine reader of his own work, not always the case with novelists), of having him expound on some element or other as he arrived at it in the writing. As the text began to accumulate, it was inspiring to hear his enthusiasm grow—he was beginning to believe that his earlier hopes for *The Last Confession* might just be realised and that it could indeed become one of his more important books. Sorrowfully, I also remember how many times he voiced the hope that he be given the strength and time to complete it.

By my estimation, we have been left with about seventy per

cent of the word extent he was working towards. This, however, is no more than an educated guess, as novels do often acquire a life of their own in the execution and can take their writer on a longer or shorter or even very different journey to the one anticipated in any planning stage. Such estimate as I can come up with is also based on the research material gathered as background and the areas covered therein.

No one can know how Morris intended to end the novel at hand. We had had no conversation on the subject. Further, the narrative method he had chosen adds its own difficulty. Just what the author was intending to light upon, to concentrate on and flesh out in the time between 4 January 1600—the last day treated in the draft—and the day of Bruno's death, is impossible to say. He may have been intending to go back to some earlier time in Bruno's life, or he may have settled into a more detailed exposition of the last days.

Finally, and for the record, it should be stated that the decision to publish an incomplete novel was one taken by Morris's family alone. They, and particularly his wife Joy, are to be thanked for allowing this to be added to Morris's record of achievement, and for allowing his countless fans around the world this last, if sad, pleasure.

Author's Note

I make no claims as to the provenance of this document. As to the authenticity of its content, I can affirm that it hews steadily to the historical line revealed in the published documents of Bruno's trials in Venice and Rome, and by the later researches of his biographers and commentators: Spampanato, Firpo, Mercati, Yates, Ciliberto and others.

The character of Bruno, herein described, is an accurate, if not always endearing, portrait of a genius, born out of due time, at odds with himself, a victim of the prejudices of his age, who at his end achieved the dignity of a martyr and an enduring place in the history of honest dissent.

I came to know him first when I stood before his great bronze image in the Campo dei Fiori in Rome, and read the dedicatory inscription: *To Giordano Bruno, from the century he guessed at, in Rome, on the place where he was burned.*

The publication of this document is my tribute to his memory on the four hundredth anniversary of his death.

Morris West
Clareville, 1999

The last confession of
Filippo Giordano Bruno
called the Nolan
written in his cell at Rome
in the last month of his life
in the year 1600

Rome: *The Prison of The Holy Office*
21 December 1599

I know this place very well. I have lived here for nearly seven years since they extradited me from Venice—a miserable winter journey which I still remember in my aching bones.

In prison one loses count of time. One tries at first to measure it by the pale light that penetrates through a high barred window. Then one abandons the effort. Why connive with the gaolers to torment oneself?

Nevertheless, I am sure of today's date because the Notary announced it when I was brought before the Congregation of the Office of the Holy Roman and Universal Inquisition.

They make an impressive assembly: nine Most Illustrious and Most Reverend Lord Cardinals, six high and reverend clerics—religious and regular—and, of course, the Notary, meticulous recorder of the proceedings, which today are minuted under the heading: Visitation of Those Incarcerated in the Holy Roman Office. I am only one of the prisoners; but today they tell me I am the sole object of my lords' attentions.

First I am required to identify myself. God! How many times have I done this? How many notaries have recorded it in how many documents? My family name is Bruno. I was born in 1548 in the city of Nola, in the kingdom of Naples. My father's name was Giovanni. My mother's name was Fraulisa. My baptismal name is Filippo. However, I am characterised in all documents by my name in religion, Giordano. I am an ordained priest, a monk in the Order of Friars Preachers, a Master in sacred theology.

Each of these titles is authentic. Each provides a separate noose to hang me. I no longer practise my ministry, therefore I am accused for my 'loose and licentious life'. I have fled my order, therefore I am an 'apostate monk'. I am accused of perverting the Divine science of theology into outright heresy. For that, they can have me executed.

Today the man who addresses me on behalf of the Inquisitors is the Illustrious and Most Reverend Lord Cardinal Robert Bellarmine, a Jesuit said to stand high in favour with the Pontiff. Unlike some of his colleagues, he is mild-mannered and courteous—though I am too old in prison life to trust him too far.

What he tells me is very simple. He and his colleagues have finished their enquiries into my life, my writings and my opinions. There will be no more interrogations. Immediately after Christmas the Congregation will make its decision. When next I am summoned it will be to hear the verdict.

Meantime—and this is the core of a very sour apple—I should use the coming weeks to reconsider my position most carefully. Bellarmine emphasises the expression with a grammarian's precision. The word *resipiscere* means to 'rethink with wisdom'.

I feel a sudden anger rising in me. What in God's name have I been doing all these years in prison but thinking and rethinking, testing one argument against another—even when my mind was fuddled with fever, my body racked with rheumatic pains? I manage to control myself and answer firmly but with respect. I have no wish and I feel no obligation to reconsider any matter. I have answered all the questions that have been put to me over months and years. I do not understand what is now expected of me.

My Lord Cardinal Bellarmine explains. He and his colleagues understand the impediment I feel. It is a state not uncommon on the difficult journey to repentance and spiritual enlightenment. For this reason they have asked the Master General of my Order and his

Vicar to meet privately with me in my cell and help me to see the vanity of my way of life and the doctrinal errors into which I have fallen. He asks whether I am prepared to receive them and reason with them openly.

Of course I am prepared to talk—anything to defer the final fateful day of decision! However, I tell him I can make no promise of change. He understands that. He even commends my honesty. Then in the same mild fashion, he reminds me that my liberty, my life and my eternal salvation all hang upon the outcome.

What can I say? I know that I am two steps away from the moment I have always dreaded. They have squeezed me like an orange, down to the pips and skin. I bow my head in silence and wait to be dismissed. To my surprise I am offered some small indulgences.

Henceforth I am to lodge alone in my cell. I am grateful for that. I have learned many times to my cost that cellmates may turn out to be informers, like that sad fellow Celestine the Capuchin who traduced me to save his own skin. He caused me months of trouble with his reports of our cell talk, and his accounts of my blasphemous and licentious mockeries. It availed him nothing. Three months ago they took him out and burned him for heresy in the Campo dei Fiori.

So my privacy is a comfort; but there is still a drop of gall in the wine cup. I know, and the Inquisitors know, that solitude breeds fear, uncertainty and doubt and nightmare terrors. I am much pleased when Bellarmine tells me that I am to be given quills and ink and paper and candles to help my failing eyesight. Again there is a dash of wormwood in the cup. I may not write any matters not connected with my case. I may not possess or read any other book than that which has been provided to me: the breviary approved for the special use of the Order of Friars Preachers. For the rest, I shall have to keep my mind alive with a daily harvest of memories.

I make bold at this point to express some simpler needs. My robe is thin and threadbare. My cell is cold as a tomb. My joints are swollen and painful, my hands raw with chilblains. I ask for a woollen robe and cloak, mittens for my hands and socks to temper the chill of the stone paving.

Some of the Inquisitors clearly disapprove these mitigations. Bellarmine reduces them swiftly to compliance. The Notary is directed to issue a procurement order to the Master of the Wardrobe. Money is provided so that I may bathe and scrub myself in heated water and pay the barber to trim my hair and beard.

I thank my lords for their indulgences. I make a final request that the order be expedited. Once the illustrious visitors have departed, prison life will resume its customary pace—promises will string themselves out into long tomorrows like beads on a long rosary.

Bellarmine accepts the plea. He turns to his colleagues and admonishes them: "It is we who control this place and not the staff. What we order should be executed without delay. And you, Brother Bruno, you too should attend instantly to your soul's wellbeing. Time passes swiftly and you are, every moment, in jeopardy. You may go now."

My gaoler walks me back to my cell and locks me in. I fling myself on my bed and huddle there like a foetus, dead in a dark womb, doomed never to see the light of day. Then, slowly, the madness of despair subsides into a cold, black anger. The anger is good. It affirms that I am alive and still unbroken. They have me caught and penned; but I am not a sheep. They shall know that I am a wolf, who can still snap and snarl and bite the hand of any intruder.

* * *

The country folk among whom I was born have an old saying: "When you start a vendetta always dig two graves." Well, it is they who have mounted a vendetta against me. They have made me a vagabond among the scholars of Europe; they have libelled me, they have deprived me of liberty; they threaten my life; they seek even to pursue me to the judgement seat of the Almighty. They have all the armoury, all the power.

The only weapons I have are those which they have decreed to me today: pens made from goose feathers, ink from soot and gall, a pile of blank paper and a month of time. What can I do with so little? Very soon my enemies will destroy me; but they, too, are mortal and will die and be buried in due time. At least I can give myself the pleasure of writing our epitaphs.

Already the superscription shapes itself in my head: *The Last Confession of Filippo Giordano Bruno, called the Nolan, who now presents himself for the judgement of history.*

What am I to tell in this writing? An epitaph, however brief, is a memorial. What do I desire most to be remembered about myself? Of what do I wish to convince those who may, in some obscure future, read it?

I shall not have time and I have in any case no inclination to write a chronicle of my life or a defence of my opinions. These have been covered—God, with what tedious repetition and elaboration!—in the records of my inquisitions in Venice and here in Rome.

Rather I should like to make known—simply and openly, as in casual discourse of friends—who I am, and how I read the destiny which has brought me to this moment. That destiny was written from the beginning on the palm of my own hand, even though I lacked the wit to read or decipher it.

I cannot set this down all in one piece, like an oration or philosopher's argument. I have walked that road before and it leads nowhere. So, the best I can offer is anecdote, allusion, scraps and shards of memory which may reveal themselves in the end as a mosaic portrait of the real Bruno who lives within my skin.

For a moment, I find a tenuous joy in the idea. Then I am stricken with a new horror: if I am condemned then I shall be stripped of every possession except my robe and delivered in chains to the commandant of Nona Tower, who will be charged to hand me in short order to the executioners.

What then will become of my manuscript? How as I write can I conceal it? How shall I get it out of here into safe and friendly hands?

All I can think at this moment is that, even in this place, strictly confined and closely guarded, I have been able to do small favours for humble people: write a note for a lovesick youth, a letter of appeal for patronage for an unlettered guard. Perhaps one of them will oblige me in my turn. For that I have to trust to luck, since, being an apostate monk and under attainder for heresy, I can hardly appeal to Divine Providence. Oh, Brother Giordano! You wrote so confidently of an infinite universe and of plural worlds beyond our view, yet you cannot control even this tiny rat-hole on your own planet.

23 December

It has taken two days, but Bellarmine has kept his promise. This morning I am permitted to bathe in a tub of tepid water. When I strip down I can count the bones in my ribcage and the wrinkles in my shrunken belly. My leg muscles are wasting for want of exercise. My skin, once the grime comes off, is pale and yellow like that of a plucked chicken.

My old clothes are taken away and fresh ones tossed on my bed. They are not new—God forbid! They are patched and darned, but at least they are clean and free of prison stink.

A barber comes to trim my hair and beard. I have not met this one before. He is curt and graceless. He talks in grunts and bursts of *Romanaccio*, a clattering dialect which falls harshly on the ear of a southerner like me, whose language is made for singing.

I ask what has happened to his colleague. He is sick. He has the *mal'aria*. When will he be back? "Who knows? It is God who arranges such things."

I am glad to see the back of this surly brute. I miss the other one who is a Neapolitan like myself, garrulous and full of gossip. He is kind, too. Sometimes he will slip me a piece of fruit or a sweetmeat, and always he has some bawdy scandal to brighten my day.

On my desk there are three candles, one in a sconce, the two others laid side by side on the desk top. I am warned that this is all I shall get until the next visit of the Inquisitors. I calculate carefully how I can make them last. If you laugh at this childish mathematic, let me remind you how precious light is, the joy it brings, the terror when you are robbed of it.

Suddenly—and not unpleasantly—I am reminded of my student days in Naples. We were a rowdy and roistering lot. Most of us were poor and we earned our money by making deliveries for shopkeepers. We paid for our pleasures by running errands for the girls in the brothels. In one of the reports on my candidacy as a novice in the Order I was called a *postiglione per le puttane:* a postillion for the whores! There was a double edge to the joke. A postillion rides the lead horse in a carriage team. The second meaning was plain. It suggested that I rode the girls as well.

I did, of course. I was a hot-blooded boy and proud of my new manhood. It seemed to please the girls, too. They told me it was a change from old fellows who took an hour to work up an erection. I remember now that the pleasure was always measured by candlelight. The candle by each girl's bed was marked by the brothel master: six sessions to an hour. If you wanted more than ten minutes, or if you needed time to get into action, you paid for it.

When you had paid your money, the girl lit the candle. When the wax melted down to the line which marked your time, the girl snuffed out the candle. The brief season of love was over. You and your credit were exhausted.

You couldn't argue about it. If you did, you took a beating and were thrown out into the street. So there is a phrase in our language: *cortigiana a candela,* a candle courtesan. And that, come to think of it, is what my Lords Inquisitors would like to make of me, measuring out my life by candle flame and melted wax.

Beside the candles there is a pile of blank paper, a pot of ink and a dozen quills already cut for writing. I prefer to cut my own to fit the shape and slant of my handwriting. In the past I have asked for a small penknife, but this has always been refused. I must not possess any instrument with which I can damage myself or others.

No matter. These few casements have already restored my self-respect and my small stock of courage. So now, I am prepared to sit down, dip quill in inkpot and begin writing my last confession.

*   *   *

My father, Giovanni, was a soldier in the service of the viceroy of Naples. Do not misunderstand me. This was no ruffian freelance selling himself to the highest bidder for any of the dirty business of soldiering. He belonged to an elite corps, one of sixteen companies, each of seventy men who were the backbone of the garrison forces of the Duke of Alba. There were strict conditions for their enlistment: they must be gentlemen born, of good appearance, healthy in body, intelligent and of proven valour. They were well paid. My father earned a stipend of eighty ducats a year, out of which he had to furnish two good horses and a groom.

In my childhood he was absent for long periods on service in the Abruzzi, Puglia and the seaboard areas threatened by corsair invasions. In my mind he was a heroic figure, a free spirit, confronting the King's enemies, travelling a world of which I knew nothing. On his rare visits home, I would plead with him to tell me stories of his campaigns, but he was a taciturn man who had no taste for storytelling. So I invented his exploits, about which I boasted to my friends.

My mother fretted over his absences and nagged him when he was at home. Looking back I can hardly blame her. She was a virtual widow and brought me up alone, although she lived in the midst of an extended family of relations. In the end she became subject to fits of melancholy which made her life and mine a domestic misery.

Even so, I did not lack company or diversion. Our house was part of the estate of the Savalino family. It was one of nine dwellings, occupied by fourteen families. We boys were taught reading and writing and simple arithmetic by a local priest, Don Gian Domenico.

When we were not in class, we roamed the countryside around the foot of the mountain which was called Cicada. It was a domain rich with olives, chestnuts, oaks, poplars, rosemary, vines, elms and myrtles.

Beyond this Eden lay the sprawling city of Naples, and beyond that—the limit of the world as I knew it—the dark and sinister cone of Vesuvius, with its plume of brown smoke, and, at night, the intermittent glow of its pulsing fiery heart.

The mystery and terror of that mountain was the beginning of all my later questionings about the nature of the world, of the universe itself, of its Maker and of our human destinies. The destruction of the cities of Pompeii and Herculaneum was still vivid in our folklore. Every preacher used it as a text, speaking of it as an act of Divine vengeance: God raining down fire on the dissolute inhabitants as once he had done upon Sodom and Gomorrah. Even then the crude proposition stuck in my gullet. When I lived in Naples as a student the notion became even less digestible. Ours was a Christian city, but it was no whit more virtuous than old Pompeii. There was just as much lust and villainy and violence as there had been among the ancients.

So there seemed no good reason why Vesuvius should not, once again, be used as an instrument of Divine punishment. All the land around the Bay of Naples from Sorrento to Pozzuoli was unstable ground, which rose and fell and sent up warning fumaroles from the fires beneath. Sometimes, after a boozy, bawdy night, I dreamed that I was choking on hot dust and noxious vapours.

Even as I write these words, the nightmare takes hold of me again. If the Inquisitors condemn me, I shall die at the stake, suffocating in the woodsmoke while the flames rise to consume me. This, too, they will call a Divine vengeance, because they claim to judge me in the name of God.

How do I judge myself? That's the core of the matter. There is no time left to cherish illusions; no illusion is worth dying for. So the question extends itself: what is illusion, what is reality?

One reality is that I am a child of the sun. I sprang from a coast where grapes grow and oranges, where the sea is warm and blue and the women are warm too, and the men are as swift to laughter as to anger.

We talk a lot and argue at the tops of our voices. We lie easily and shrug when we are caught out—which is the way of subject people with their conquerors. Yet we are just as vain as any of the Spanish magnificoes who strutted our streets as if they owned them—which indeed they did, since we were ruled from Spain by a Spanish viceroy. Yet the city was always rebellious—a pebble in the boot of Italy.

In our student days we all carried arms. There were many affrays in the university itself, on the stairs, in the courtyards, even in the Church of San Domenico. In the end, harsh penalties were proclaimed against disturbers of the peace: four hoists on the rope to dislocate your shoulders, with further penalties for repeat offenders: for nobles, banishment; for commoners, compulsory service chained to the oars in the galleys.

I was lucky enough to stay out of serious trouble. I was much happier to tumble a girl than stand in an alley with dagger drawn against the bullies. Besides, for a man of my condition, a soldier's son, with no title of nobility and no large prospect of inheritance, learning was the only road to advancement, and the Church was the door that opened directly on to that highway.

I studied theology with Mattia Gibbonis, Ambrogio da Nopoli and Giacomo Marotta—all Dominicans. I read metaphysics with Agostino Manualdo and with Geronimo de Cardines, who was an Augustinian. They were all monks and, like assiduous gardeners training a vine to a trellis, they bent my growing mind to religion.

I could not claim to be pious, but my teachers knew—or thought they knew—what could be made of youths like me: ambitious for learning, but without resources and vulnerable to the turbulent world around us. The life of a regular religious offered not only material security, but a place in the established order of things, and the opportunity to rise step by step to eminence and authority within that order. Not all of this was clear to me at the time, but the understanding was filtered to me slowly by my mentors. One day perhaps I might qualify for admission to the Order of Friars Preachers in the local community of San Domenico.

It seemed that I had at least some of the necessary qualities: I was of legitimate birth, well educated, instructed in grammar, unmarried, free from any hidden illnesses. The excesses of my student life were no impediment. They could be expunged in the general confession which would precede my entry—and the Master of Novices would lead or drive me along the upward path to virtue.

There was much to recommend the notion: a full belly, a protected and studious life, a chance to quit before I took vows and was ordained a priest. Could I live celibate? I thought so. Life with my mother had given me no taste at all for marriage. Chastity was another matter altogether; but the tolerances of the time, if not the ideal of the founding father, Saint Dominic, might make its practice less arduous. Besides, I had already discovered that serious study did alleviate some of the pangs of desire. Indeed, one of the girls whom I frequented—a dark lively little thing whose mother was Moorish—used to tell me: "I always know when you are studying, Filippo. You work us both too hard, and it's only half the fun!"

But why waste paper and precious candlelight on this lost time? On the fifteenth day of June in the year of our Lord 1565, I received the tonsure of a minor cleric and put on the habit of a Dominican monk. I also assumed a new name, to symbolise my new identity: Giordano.

There now, I know I've got the date right this time. When I was questioned in Venice seven years ago, I got it wrong and the error was never corrected. As if it mattered an owl's hoot! My entry into religion was the first step towards the damnation with which the Lords Inquisitors threaten me now: for my body, death by fire; for my soul an eternity of torment. This is the nature of the madness they propagate: to make a man confess a loving God, you burn him!

Enough for now. I rearrange my papers, putting the sheets I have written at the bottom of the pile. I clean my quills and stretch myself out on my bed to compose myself for the visit of the Master General and his Vicar.

They make a curious pair: the Master General, tall, lean, with piercing eyes set in a visage that might have been carved from old wood; the Vicar, round and ruddy as an apple, but watchful and deferential always to the Master. Their greeting is cool. They are clearly uncomfortable in my narrow room with its pervasive smell of mouldy stone, Tiber damp and stale urine. Even the Master General seems at a loss for words to open the dialogue. I wait in respectful silence. Finally, he speaks.

"I am glad, Brother Giordano, that you are prepared to treat openly with us. You know that we are here to help you—if you will allow us."

"I am in great need of help, Master. May I ask some questions first?"

"By all means."

"In terms of the law, I am still bound by my vows, yes?"

"You are, both legally and morally."

"Therefore I am still under the jurisdiction of the Order—your jurisdiction, Master."

"In strict legality you have passed into the jurisdiction of the Inquisitors, but I remain your religious superior."

"So, how do you see me? As a brother or an enemy?"

He takes a little time to frame the answer, but his tone is mild.

"I see you as a brother who has wandered too long and too far from our Father's house."

"And if I return repentant, you will receive me with joy and kill the fatted calf?"

The Vicar opens his mouth to speak, but the Master General checks him with a gesture.

"I am not your father, I am your brother. Our common father on earth is His Holiness, who speaks for our Father in heaven. It is for him to say whether or no you may be welcomed back into his house. Only he can dispense you from your solemn vows or the censures under which you lie at this moment."

"I know that, Master General. I have presented several petitions for clemency directly to His Holiness. I am assured that they were delivered. I am also told that His Holiness has refused even to open them. Can you tell me why?"

"His Holiness has decided in his wisdom that he will not intervene. He will leave the determination of the case to the tribunal of the Most Holy Inquisition."

"In short then, I remain a prisoner in our Father's house. I am not a returning prodigal, but for ever an outcast."

"That is not yet decided, Brother." Now finally the Vicar has found voice—light and high like a castrate tenor. "The tribunal is still considering its verdict."

"So tell me, gentlemen, please, what is the point of this conversation?"

I look from one to the other. The Vicar is studying the cracks in the pavement of my cell. The eyes of the Master are filmed like those of a hawk before it is loosed from the jess. His voice has now a razor edge to it.

"Our concern, Brother, is not the verdict of the Inquisitors. They will deliver that in due course. Sentence will be passed. The Holy Father will approve whatever is done. We are here as your brothers, to help you to repentance, offer you absolution, and reconcile you with the Church and with God. If you choose to see it aright, this is a moment of grace. Whatever happens to you afterwards, you will accept as the thief on the cross accepted to die beside the Saviour and was welcomed into paradise by him. Do you understand what I am saying to you?"

Do I understand? Sweet suffering Christ! For a moment reason lurches towards madness. I have heard all this before, and I still gag on the reverent hypocrisies.

Extra ecclesia nulla salus. Outside the Church there is no salvation. Millions of human souls, made, they say, in the image of God, tumble every day into damnation like leaves in an autumn wind. The keys to the kingdom of heaven are held by a man who declines to open his correspondence—not to mention his heart. I have no hope of reaching him. The adits to his house are guarded by the hounds of God, ready to harry and tear all intruders. The Master and the Vicar are watching me closely, waiting upon my answer. I give it as calmly as I can.

"I am grateful for your goodwill, Master General. I am touched by your concern for my soul's wellbeing. I am not sure how much either will avail me if the Inquisitors convict me and His Holiness turns his face away."

"But God will never turn away from the penitent sinner. His mercy is infinite."

"Then why do I find so little in His Church?"

"That is blasphemy!" The Vicar is vehement in protest and suddenly all my calm is lost. I shout at him.

"No, Vicar! No! No! No! You are the ones who commit the blasphemies—arrest without charge, witnesses without names, confessions extracted by torture, conviction without appeal. How can we believe in the God you display to us?"

Suddenly, I find myself weeping: great racking sobs that seem to tear my breast apart. I bury my face in my hands. I pull away violently when the Master General lays a hand on my shoulder. His voice echoes far away, a Delphic utterance from a dark cave.

"Let the tears flow, Brother. Let the grace of God work its healing in you."

When I look up, they are gone. When I have wept myself out I am ashamed that they have seen me like this. The surge of black rage that follows is the true mercy. I am not broken yet. I still possess the small core of myself: Filippo Giordano Bruno called the Nolan.

24 December

Today is the eve of the Nativity: the birthday of our Lord and Saviour Jesus Christ. The phrase runs smoothly from my pen. It is familiar and definitive. One could begin a history with it, or make a sermon on it like one of those I used to make as a new young priest in the Church of San Domenico in Naples. That was twenty-three years ago—nearly a quarter of a century.

Now the meaning of the words has changed for me. How can I call Jesus 'my Lord' when his Vicar on earth rejects me and his servants cast me out of the house? How can I call him 'Saviour' when the writ of condemnation which may be issued against me runs past the frontier of time and into eternity? *Whatsoever you shall bind or loose on earth shall be bound or loosed in heaven.*

This, they claim, is the power of the keys given by Christ to Peter, transmitted down the centuries to those who follow Peter in lawful succession. But is it truly so; or is it, as the Greeks have always claimed, an exaggerated interpretation by the Romans to bolster their authority? It makes no matter now. Whatever I say, and even what I am deemed to think, will be imputed as heresy.

I turn away from these sterile deserts of argument and bask for a while in the sunlit meadows of my childhood in Nola.

Today, in every church in the kingdom of Naples, they will be setting up the *presepio*, the crib: the group of figures representing the Christ-child, sleeping in a manger, with Mary and Joseph and the shepherds attending on him, while the animals, an ox, an ass, a sheep, breathe warmth into the winter air. Some of these figures are very old, beautifully carved by local craftsmen, lovingly displayed to each generation.

Even I, the sceptic without illusions, the doubter whose brain-box buzzes with unanswered questions, am moved by the simplicity of the scene. I make no mockeries here. I yearn for the peace which abides in the humble shelter of the stable.

To us in the south, the cycle of birth, death and continual renewal is commonplace but still a mysterious marvel. Fruitful woman is a goddess figure, precious and sacred. We tyrannise our wives and our sisters; but we honour them, too. Our grandmothers become matriarchs, not to be gainsaid. Even in the bloodiest vendettas, the women of the families are untouchable. It is not so with those who by fault or default are regarded as dishonoured, because they have lost their maidenheads outside of marriage.

I understand this in my bones. I understand also the doctrine of the virginity of Mary, which I am claimed to have rejected. The maiden mother is among the most ancient figures in Mediterranean legend, but you have to accept her and not argue about her in the manner of the schoolmen. You cannot prove her by texts and syllogisms.

I will admit that I fell into this trap in some of my early disputations: in my talk with Mocenigo, and in the ribald exchanges with fellow prisoners in Venice. In prison, as on the battlefield, bawdy talk is a defence against madness. My own memory is that I was mimicking the old-fashioned Aristotelian debates—of which I became a dangerously adept satirist. What was reported to the Inquisition, however, was something different, a bald proposition: it is a nonsense to claim that a virgin, without a man to seed her, can beget a child.

How do you rebut an accusation like that, especially when your accuser is still unnamed and you cannot confront him to show a true colouration of the words and the occasion? Besides, the presumption of the Inquisitors is always that the accused is guilty until the contrary is proven. So I languish in prison, while the principal witness remains at liberty.

I muse again on the images of the *presepio*: Saint Joseph, who we were taught was the foster father of Jesus. Our images show him always as an older man, a protector, but not a marriage partner of Mary. Truth or legend? It is truth because the Church is said always to have taught it. Yet the Apostle James is always referred to as the Brother of the Lord. Other family members are mentioned but not named. Our masters performed all kinds of acrobatics to explain these references, and we were not encouraged to make controversy about them, even in rhetorical debate. One of my most respected teachers, Vincenzo Colle, called the Sarnese, put it neatly: "The gift of faith does not necessarily include the gift of certainty. It is an act of assent. Remember that always, Brother Giordano." It was good advice. I wish to God I had taken more heed of it.

The thought of sexual relations raises poignant memories. This will be the bleakest Christmas of my life. I find myself longing for the warmth of a woman's body in my bed. I am accused—justly, I admit—of being a fugitive monk and a profligate priest, but there are so many of both these days, I cannot see that I should be a prime candidate for execution. The pontiffs who have reigned in my lifetime have not all been models of chaste virtue.

When the Inquisitors laid these charges against me, I had no choice but to plead myself guilty, offering in defence that unchastity in this day and age was at worst a venial offence, and that my flight from the convent was promoted by fear. In Naples, I was arraigned for trial on a false imputation of heresy. I knew how the Inquisition worked—it is we Dominicans who are appointed to run it! So I was afraid. I fled.

I was learning very fast in those early days of confinement in Venice. The first lesson was not to show too brave a face under torture.

That only encouraged the fellows administering it to work harder on the hoist. So I let out screams and shouts at the top of my voice. The hurt was the same, but the duration, usually a half-hour session of *strappado* before the interrogation, was not unduly prolonged.

I was slower to learn the second lesson: that the Inquisitors took a milder view of personal delinquencies than of any slurs or imputations against the Church, its ministers or its doctrines. They understood very well that I, Brother Giordano, was no threat: I was a nobody who could be crushed like a flea. But ideas are another matter. They are dragon seed, blown hither and yon by every wind, which one day may spring up armed men. So they have winnowed me, year after year, to separate the poison grain and burn it.

This, you see, was at once my vanity and my simplicity. I was a country boy born into a new world, turbulent, yes, but still full of wonders. I was full of questions about everything. I was told I lacked humility to learn from great masters. Perhaps I did, but they lacked the skill to touch my heart and profit from my curiosity.

My contacts with women were frequent and for the most part pleasant, but my attachments were always brief. A man like me, without permanence or patronage, was never a welcome suitor in any father's house. Clerics and scholars always travelled light. No matter how much learning they carried in their heads, there was little gold in their saddlebags. So my loves were, for the most part, candle courtesans, or tavern girls, or unhappy wives or widows, glad of any comfort in their beds. There were enough of them all so that I could boast, out of prison and inside it, that while I could not match King Solomon's lovers, I thought I could run him close.

It is the boasting that has always undone me. In any debate or discussion, I have to top the argument. In any game of wit, I must deliver the last word in satire or invective. The need that betrays me is to assert the real Bruno, concealed, overlaid, suppressed by the habit I assumed too readily with too shallow a conviction.

In bed with a willing woman, I have never needed to boast. I have not demanded to prove myself upon her, only to enjoy and be enjoyed. Yet even in this, I have damaged my cause. It was no boast but simple exuberance when I declared: "The Church is wrong to make a sin of what serves men and women so well and pleasantly."

If only I had put it another way—left out the Church and found another word for sin—this charge would never have been read into the indictment. But I was a priest and teacher, charged to spread the Gospel truth, pure and undefiled. I was, moreover, a Dominican, one of the hounds of God, an Inquisitor in embryo no less!—so they judged me the more harshly. To the devil with them, and all their systems and syllogisms.

In the darkness of my cell, I call up by name and face and from remembered touch, all the women I have ever known—and even those I have not dared to know, like the ladies-in-waiting at the court of Queen Elizabeth of England, or the sad but beautiful young wife of Giovanni Mocenigo, who befriended me during my ill-fated sojourn in his house. They parade before me to the music of a slow pavane, a vision of fair ladies, briefly possessed, lost a long time. They stir me still but, satirist that I am, I ask myself how I would perform if by a miracle any one of them came into my cell.

I am still toying with the thought when Rome breaks out with a tumult of bells to toll the hour of midnight and announce the birthday of Christ.

25 December

Feast of The Nativity

In the forenoon, my cell door is opened and the guard ushers in a visitor. He is a little man, half a head shorter than I—and I am a small-boned southerner. He is also at least twenty years older. His face is seamed and wrinkled like the skin of a very old apple. His dead-white hair is thin and wispy, but his eyes are cornflower blue and there is a sparkle of mischief in them. He is dressed in the habit of Saint Dominic which falls about him in a shapeless mass. He addresses me in Latin: the Latin of our daily commerce in school and lecture hall and academic intercourse. However, his accent falls strangely on my ears as he explains himself.

"I am Brother John. If I look strange to you it is because I am strange. The Father General calls me his *homunculus Britannicus*, his English dwarf, because I was a member of the Black Friars community in London. I had to leave in a hurry because I was being dogged by the pursuivants of Sir Francis Walsingham. That was just after you arrived and took up residence with the French Ambassador. I have to say I envied you then, Brother Giordano. You were living in very grand style while I was hiding with the families of Catholic merchants trading across the channel."

"So perhaps you will tell me, good Brother John, what brings you here today?"

"At this point in my career—which is certain to go down, rather than up—I serve as almoner to the Master General."

I gape at him in disbelief. "I have been in prison here for nearly seven years. No one of my brethren has offered me a gift or a comfort in all that time."

"Then allow me to change the custom."

With that, he hoists up the skirt of his gown and discloses a piece of fisherman's net threaded about his skinny waist. The net is full of wonders: a jar of pickled olives, a round of good goat cheese, a big country sausage, a flask of red wine, another of strong fruit liquor, a loaf of wheaten bread, two oranges, two apples and a bag of sugared almonds. These are treasures more precious than diamonds, yet I burst out laughing. There is something gloriously comic in this little dwarfish fellow waddling around Rome with a whole larder slung around his middle. He laughs, too, and begins unloading the cargo, talking as he goes.

"If I carried them in a basket, I should be paying tribute at every step: to the watch, to the guards at the gate, to the fellow who opens your cell. You know how it goes in this town."

"I should, but I am not much abroad, as you know. But this, this is a miracle!"

"I am told—gossip only from the tribunal, of course—that you proclaimed openly that all miracles were conjuring tricks."

"It's part of my problem. I open my mouth too wide in the wrong company."

"Now there's a truth! But this, dear Brother, is explainable by natural causes, so by definition it cannot be a miracle."

"So explain the natural causes."

"For that we need to stimulate the brain."

He hoists up his skirts again and produces yet another flask, already uncorked. This time it is grappa and clearly it is for his own use against the winter cold. Again, I have a comical vision: the little man hoisting his habit to piddle in a shadowy corner of the city, holding his penis with one hand and pouring liquor down his throat with the other. I am reminded of the Emperor Augustus and his nickname for the poet Horace: *peniculus meus,* my little prick. I smile at the memory. Brother John demands that I share the joke. I can hardly refuse.

Much to my surprise he laughs too. He reaches for my drinking cup and pours me a generous measure of the fiery liquor. Then, he tells me: "There's nothing more pleasant than completing the circle—pouring good liquor in at one end and still being able to piss comfortably at the other. A rare gift at my age, believe me! But there is one small problem."

"And what, pray, is that?"

"A good woman passes—worse still, an innocent maid. She curtseys and begs a blessing. What do I do? My left hand holds the bottle. My right, the blessing hand, holds my limp member. Not an edifying spectacle!"

We laugh together. I try to discern what lies behind those twinkling blue eyes. I press the question.

"Who sent these gifts and why?"

"The who is easy: the Master General himself."

"And the why?"

"That needs a little explaining." He pours a grappa down his gullet. "It happened yesterday. The Master and his Vicar had returned from their visit to you. They were talking with three or four members of the chapter. You were discussed very briefly and dismissed with a gesture. The Master General said, 'We have broken him, I think. I shall visit him again after Epiphany.' Mention of that feast raised the much more important matter of alms and gifts to friends of the Order. In Rome, tribute is paid up and down the line. It is my task to see that no one is forgotten, especially any who might harm us or hold a grudge. I had read through my list. The Master asked whether there was anyone we had forgotten. Then, not without certain mischief, I asked, 'Should we not perhaps provide a small gift for Brother

Giordano?' The others burst into laughter. I thought I should get a reprimand if not a penance from the Master. Instead, he rounded on the other brethren and gave them a tongue-lashing: 'Brother John is right,' he said. 'We spent a long time yesterday trying to persuade Brother Giordano to repentance for his misdeeds. If a small act of charity will help him to that saving act, we should not withhold it. See to it, Brother John. Food and drink for the feast day will serve him best, I think. He's as thin as a broom handle.' The other friars were still digesting their reproof. One of them asked finally: 'Does this mean a pardon for all his misdeeds and heresies?' The Master's answer was instant and precise. 'In the forum of the sacrament, yes. Given the right disposition of his soul, we offer him absolution, the Eucharist and the Last Anointing. Then we hand him, purged of his sins, to the civil authority who, in punishment for his crimes, will despatch him to God. That is the law. There is no appeal from it unless the Pope decrees otherwise—which he has no disposition to do at this moment.'"

And this is how my sentence is delivered to me, a month in advance of the formal verdict. It is offered with wine and food, as if I am an angry demon who must be placated. Yet, suddenly, there is no anger left in me. This odd little man with his cornflower eyes and his limping Latin speech is one of God's good men—if God is making good men anymore! He waits for me to say something. I tell him I feel like getting drunk, which I have not done for many years. I offer to break out one of my own bottles and share the bread and sausage with him. He shakes his head.

"Save them, Brother. Don't drink all the liquor at once. That will leave you with a headache which, with all your other troubles, you need not at all. It will also give the guards an excuse to steal your food. Take my advice, enjoy a little wine every day. Make the good things last. Would you feel badly if I said a prayer for you—very short, just a Pater and Ave?"

"You're a free man, Brother John. Pray or not as you choose. In my mouth at this moment the words would be a blasphemy."

He stretches out to clasp and hold my trembling hand. His

grip is surprisingly strong. Then, quietly and intimately, he murmurs the prayers.

"*Pater noster qui es in coelis…*"

I seal my lips but I cannot stop my ears. The old voice murmurs on. The grip on my hand is strong but comforting. I surrender my mind to the familiar cadences, as to a song without words, but the very last line of the prayer hits me like a hammer blow.

"…*et ne nos inducas in tentationem*"—and spare us the testing time.

My testing time is now a certainty, written into the lines of my palm, never to be erased. When Brother John invokes the Virgin Mother, I find myself making a silent, helpless cry to my own long-lost mother.

"*Sancta Maria, Mater Dei, ora pro nobis…*"—Holy Mary, mother of God, pray for us sinners now and at the hour of our death.

To that, at least, I can say a fervent amen. What it will avail me, who knows? When the prayer is done, I thank the little man for his gifts, his company and, yes, even for his prayers. It is only then that I dare to ask him the question.

"Tell me truly, Brother John, what brought you to me?"

He hesitates a moment, then gives me the answer.

"They could burn me, too, for what I tell you, Brother Giordano, but I hate the trade in which too many of our brethren engage themselves. To preserve the faith, which is a formula of words covering a mystery, we destroy men and women. You are my brother, more so perhaps now in your extremity than you can ever believe. God keep you. Now, hide all that stuff before I call the gaoler!"

I make haste to bury the treasures he has brought me under my tumbled blanket. It is no real hiding place but they are so sure of me now, they do not search my cell anymore. Even so, Brother John puts his hand over the spy hole in the door to block the view of any passing official. Then, when he sees me safe, he hammers on the door to summon the gaoler.

His last gesture is one of blessing, his last word a call to courage.

"*Sursum Corda.* Let us lift up our hearts." Then he is gone and I am locked once more into my solitude with only my papers, and the miraculous gifts of liquor to solace me.

The next moment is strange: a bleak calm, a cold light of revelation like sunlight on an icy mountain. It is my own tongue which has talked me into this jeopardy. My own feet have walked me into this prison. The terms of my indictment have been written by my own hand.

When I was still an infant at the breast, my parents and my godparents made on my behalf affirmations of Christian belief, and renounced on my behalf Satan and all his works. The priest poured water on my head, and then, without my knowledge or personal consent, I was baptised a Christian. I was, in the same moment, made subject to the jurisdiction of the Church and its plenary powers in the here and the hereafter.

Later, when I joined the Order of Friar Preachers and was ordained a priest, I committed myself formally by solemn vows to a completely closed system of law, of belief, even of language. The closure was formalised by a papal bull, issued by Pope Pius IV at the end of the Council of Trent, which forbade any attempt by any person 'to publish in any form, any commentaries, glosses, annotations, scholia or any kind of interpretation whatsoever, of the decrees of the said council.'

I was fifteen years old when that decree was promulgated. I had no idea—how could I?—how long and potent its consequences could be in my own life. I know now, God help me!

I am bound, beyond appeal, by the codex of canon law and the constitutions of my Order. I am required to subscribe not only to the primal Gospel truths, but to every interpretation of them by Roman authority, every expression of them in the crabbed Latin of the schoolmen. I am told what books I may read and what I am forbidden to read or to possess. The history I have been taught is expurgated and often falsified. The model for all philosophers is Aristotle. The teacher of purest theology is Aquinas—even though at the end of his life he dismissed his own work with contempt: "All

I have written is straw!" In this manifold bondage I grew very soon restless and discontented.

A monastery is a special little world, shut in behind stone walls. Amongst its inhabitants you may find a few saints, others who live in simple righteousness and others—more than the Church is willing to admit—who would sell their sisters, rob the poor box or sodomise an acolyte if the occasion offered. In this special world, there are no women, only men, who can and do grow rank with their own seed and then, like bulls penned in the same pasture, vent their rage on one another.

The conduct of the community of San Domenico was so scandalous and violent that it was forbidden, under pain of excommunication, to discuss it outside. Inevitably, because I am by nature combative and satirical, I made enemies and their enmity expressed itself by official delations to the Prior. It was prescribed by rule that we should report the delinquencies of our brethren. Specifically, I was charged with heretical leanings, because I disparaged the wearing of medallions of the Virgin and the saints as a primitive and superstitious practice, and, more seriously, because I was in possession of the commentaries of Erasmus of Rotterdam on the works of Saint John Chrysostom and Saint Jerome. Access to the writings of Erasmus was forbidden. I hid the copies in our privy, where they were later discovered and traced to me, because I had quoted from them in debates with colleagues and with visiting scholars from other convents of the Order. The climax came when the Prior told me a juridical process would be mounted against me by the Order. This was too much. I felt like a very small Daniel in a den of very large lions. So I fled.

At first, I had no clear idea of where I should go, or what I should do when I got there. All I knew was that I had to get as far as possible from Naples and from the jurisdiction of Rome and the ever-present baying hounds of God, my own brothers in religion.

I know now that I was a fool. I should have stayed and faced down my accusers, but once on the road I surrendered to the sweet illusion of liberty. It was not too hard to survive. To simple folk, I was a holy man because I wore the habit of religion. To the more educated, layman or cleric, I was a personage to be treated with respect and discreetly endowed with alms and hospitality. There was an irony in the thought: the aura of the Inquisition protected the very man it threatened!

At home in San Domenico I was missed, of course. Enquiries were begun; but I was on the move every day, travelling at least as fast as any courier.

When I met on the road or in post houses members of my own Order, I bridled my garrulous tongue, retreated behind a wall of official mystery by day and laughed into my pillow at night.

I am not laughing now. The only place where I can range freely is the countryside of memory. The only court to which I can appeal is the forum of my own conscience. But the taste of freedom is still on my tongue, the dust of many roads on my boots. I have lived in many countries: France and England and Germany and Switzerland. I have made friends in high places: nobles, princes and even a king. My voice has been heard in many halls of learning. I hope the books I have written will survive me—not even the Holy Roman Inquisition can burn them all. My folly is plain: one day, trusting in friendship, in the patronage of a powerful noble—and yes, in the validity of what I had written and the wisdom of those who might read it—I walked blithely back into captivity.

Since then, I have explored every alleyway in the labyrinth of the law seeking an exit. Every one ends in a blank wall.

When Brother John left me I sank immediately into a black pool of misery. Now truly I was bereft of hope—even of anger at what I saw as a judicial treachery. In Venice, I had made a general recantation of whatever errors I might have committed in speech or writing. This recantation had been made on a promise of liberty from the local tribunal of the Inquisition. Then the Romans had demanded my extradition, claiming that the Venetian process was only part of ongoing cases from Naples.

In Rome, many times during the years, they had offered the same bargain: recant and be free. Now they had shifted ground again. I could recant and be absolved in the forum of conscience, but I would still fall under the penalties of the law, because the Pope would not lift the censures against me. My fate was already determined. All they had to do was declare it formally with a notarised document.

Suddenly, a new impulse took hold of me. I would spread out all the food and wine and gorge myself into stupor, then let the gaolers deal with the bloated mess of Filippo Giordano Bruno the Nolan. Sanity did not return until I was setting out the food on my desk. I realised that this gluttonous folly would be the ultimate defeat for me, the ultimate victory for them. Then, indeed, the Master General could claim that he had broken me and that my weak will was evidence also of my bad faith in all my long dealings with the Inquisitors. I could not, I would not, hand them so easy a triumph.

Then the *furbizia,* the street cunning of my Neapolitan youth, offered me a small hope. Instead of filling my belly with food that would sicken me, why not use it as a bribe to gain the favour of my gaoler? One day soon, I would need a courier to take my last testament out of this prison, before I, the writer, was blotted out of the book of the living.

I had not, nor have I now, any certainty, but a long-odds gamble seems better than a glutton's bellyache. So, I batter on the door and shout for the gaoler. He takes his time coming and demands truculently to know what I want. I tell him I want the pleasure of offering him a small gift for the feast day. This persuades him to open the door and set a cautious foot within my cell.

He is young, this one, heavy jowled, dull eyed and more than a little stupid. He tells me he is alone on watch until sunset. All his colleagues are at home with their families. He demands to see the gift I have for him. I draw him inside and make sure the door is closed behind him. Then I point to the food and liquor. He gapes at it and demands to know how I came by such things. I explain. I tell him I would like him to share it with me and keep the leavings for himself. He cannot understand why I am so generous. I tell him I have small appetite these days. I have more need of company than of food. He is clearly uneasy. I urge him gently, "Please, do me this kindness. You're alone. I'm alone. Who's to know?"

It takes him a moment or two to work out this piece of mathematics. Finally, he consents. He perches himself on my stool while I stand to pour the liquor and borrow his knife to cut the bread and the sausage. The fruit and the sugared almonds I have kept hidden under my blanket—small delicacies which are no incitement to gluttony or drunkenness.

I pour myself a small careful measure of liquor, but I encourage my guest to eat and drink freely. After a while, he begins to relax. I ask about his family. His father is dead. He lives at home with his mother and an unmarried sister who, because she has no dowry, is hard to place in the marriage market. She is not bad looking, so the mother is trying to arrange a match with an elderly shopkeeper, recently widowed, who needs a woman, preferably a young woman, to look after him and the shop.

Speaking personally—he is now ready to offer confidences—he wouldn't bet on his sister's chances. There's too much competition, and a prosperous shopkeeper doesn't need to marry to have his bed warmed and his shop kept tidy!

That prompts me to ask him how the staff are betting on the outcome of my case. He shakes his head.

"Even money. That's the best anyone is offering. Unless, of course," he cocks a leery eye at me, "unless these gifts mean better news. Are they offering you perhaps a pardon in return for a name or two?"

"I doubt it, my friend."

"I wish you luck anyway. This is good sausage, good wine, too."

"Nothing but the best for the Master's table."

"How come you can be so cheerful?"

"Would it help if I wept all day?"

"I suppose not, but aren't you scared?"

"Sometimes."

"Have you ever seen a burning?"

He asks the question with a certain doltish innocence. I tell him no. It's not a spectacle I would seek out for pleasure.

"I've seen one. That fellow who shared your cell, the bearded friar, what was his name?"

"Brother Celestine."

"That's right. I went with my friend, Ambrogio. They did Celestine at night in the Campo dei Fiori. The stake was set up right opposite the French Embassy. The Ambassador made quite a fuss about it. He said the noise and the stink kept him awake, but it was quite a show, like a carnival really."

In spite of myself I am fascinated to hear his version of the event. He describes it as a child might describe a performance of Pulcinèlla at a country fair.

"First there's a procession from Nona Tower to the Campo. There's a guard of pikemen and a trumpeter. The fellow for the stake is set on a donkey. They tie his feet under the beast's belly and his hands under its neck so he won't topple off. They've dressed him in a big canvas sack painted with devils and the flames of hell. All you can see is his head. They shove a wedge of wood in his mouth so he can't curse or scream… Before the procession moves off, the mercy men take their places beside the animal."

The mercy men? It's a phrase I've never heard. I ask him who they are. He stumbles over the big word and the unusual title. It turns out that the mercy men are members of the Confraternity of San Giovanni Decollato: Saint John the Beheaded. They accompany the victim to the stake, praying, shoving a crucifix under his nose, begging him to repent before he is burned on earth and in hell. I am fascinated and revolted by this barbaric mummery. For the first time I perceive the full horror of the Gospel narrative of the crucifix-ion—Jesus nailed naked to a cross alongside two other victims, and assailed by the mockeries of a crowd and the challenges of orthodox believers to make a miracle and save himself. My storyteller is caught up in the climax of his own macabre story.

"When they get to the Campo, everything is ready. The brush-wood and pine logs are piled around the stake, doused with oil to make them burn better. They cut the fellow free from the donkey and peel him naked, like an orange. The mercy men make one last try for his soul. He turns away from them. So then he's tied to the stake and the torchbearers light the fire. I kept waiting for the fellow to scream, but of course he couldn't, with the gag in his mouth. He couldn't move much anyway because the bonds were too tight. My friend, Ambrogio, said if he was lucky he'd stifle on the smoke before the fire really got to him. Who knows? We were hemmed in by the crowd and the smoke was very thick before the flames took hold. But hell! Why am I telling you all this? It could happen to you and there's no point in going through it twice over, is there? You did say I could keep the rest of the wine and the food?"

"Please! Take it all, with my compliments."

"You're a generous man."

I shrug and force a smile, and pile the food into his arms and hold the door open for him. I cannot find words to tell him that, at this moment, another mouthful would choke me.

When darkness comes, I light one of my precious candles and draw my paper towards me and try to write the nightmares out of my brain. Try as I will, I cannot purge them. *Timor mortis conturbat me.* The fear of death terrifies me, and yet it is not so much the fear of death, it is the terrible buffoonery that accompanies it. They will make me a clown before I die…

Finally, weariness does what thinking cannot do. I sit here staring at the candle flame flickering on the blank paper, while I brush my lips with the feather of the quill.

The notion of peeling a man naked reminds me that I still have my orange. I am tempted to eat it. Instead, I hold it in my hands like a golden orb, and I understand by a strange inversion of reason that this is why they want to kill me.

The orange is their model of the universe, a sphere, complete, enclosed, requiring a prime mover to set it rolling, as I roll it with my finger across my desk. What I see is different: a cosmos expanding to infinities of earths and suns and galaxies of stars beyond our conception. The God who made it is not a juggler of celestial oranges, dazzling us with spheres in orbit. He is in all things, with all things, in us and around us, so that truly in Him we live and move and have our being. Why do they call this a heresy? Why are they set upon burning me for it?

That question, like my orange, will keep for another day. Before I quench the candle flame, I bow my head and make a prayer: "O God, if God there be, grant me for this one night a sleep without nightmares."

26 December

Feast of Saint Stephen, Martyr

My prayer for a night without dreams was granted. I slept until I was wakened by the guard, who brought my morning collation and walked with me while I emptied my bucket into the sewer hole. I found a certain irony in the fact that this one was groaning in the grip of a hangover that I myself might have had. There was another small profit: he would not bother me again until the next mealtime. I could write in peace. I could look backward to my days of liberty and not forward to my very short future.

The journey from Naples to Rome in the February of 1576 took me five days. I travelled by the historic route: Capua, Gaeta, Terracina, Velletri. Arrived in Rome, I took a big risk. I sought lodging in the convent of my Order at Santa Maria sopra Minerva. I had to know whether the news of my flight from Naples had yet reached the city. Clearly it had not, but it might arrive any day. I invented a story about a special commission from the Prior in Naples to prepare a study on the art of memory.

This, however, was too fragile a tale to hold up for long. To make matters worse, one of the brethren, involved in an affray, killed a man and tossed the body into the Tiber. I had nothing to do with the incident, but I was a newcomer in the city and therefore a natural target of suspicion. The risks were now too great. I moved again, this time divesting myself of the habit and taking on the sober dress of a scholar and carrying a sword and dagger for protection against ruffians on the road.

Now I had to begin to live on my own resources, which at that time consisted of a very small reserve of money, a stock of clerical learning, and my own talents, which were still untested in any market. I went first to Noli, an obscure little port in the territory of Genoa, the city which the great Andrea Doria had built into a maritime republic of merchants and bankers and seafarers who, following Cristoforo Colombo, opened the sea routes and became brokers of the trade with the New World. Spain was the overlord here, not Rome. There was wealth aplenty but small patronage for an obscure scholar like myself. I made a pittance teaching astronomy to certain gentlemen and grammar to snot-nosed boys. Soon I was back on the road, heading east again, Savona, Turin and across the Po valley to Venice.

There I met some Dominican friars who persuaded me that, since I was not yet excommunicated, I would be safer wearing the habit again. This involved yet another stratagem. I told the Provincial Prior, Remigio Nannisi Fiorentino, that I wanted to write and publish a book to be called 'The Signs of the Times'. He encouraged me and paid me a stipend to work on it. He was a humane man, an enlightened scholar, who was happy to take me at face value—until he saw my other face.

Once again, my southern temperament was my undoing. People were troubled by my restless questions and my constant debate. They reminded me that this was a town where secret denunciations were common: someone slipped a note into the Lion's Mouth, and before very long you were picked up by the watch for questioning and you could end hanging by the heels in the Piazzetta. Prior Remigio was a wise man. He put the money in my purse and told me I needed to travel more to observe more signs of the times. So, once again I took to the road, westward this time to Padua, Brescia, Bergamo and over the Mount Cenis Pass to Chambéry in France.

When I look back at the man I was in those first fugitive years, I am not very proud of him. He was a whirligig creature, now up, now down, spinning like a top, looking backwards, forwards and round about, all in the same moment. He was a monk, a priest, a scholar and fortune's fool as well. He wore the monkish habit like a costume for a masque. He was a priest without a congregation, a scholar without a patron who had set himself at odds with the most powerful and wealthy of all patrons: the Holy Roman, Catholic and Apostolic Church. He was an opportunist, shameless in his stratagems for survival, a braggart with nothing to boast about, because he had accomplished nothing.

Yet, there was another Bruno whom I can remember still with affection, with respect, and forgiveness for his most egregious follies. This one was still a young man with a head full of dreams jostling and shouting for release. All the voices of the age, old and new, echoed inside his skull, even though he could put no words to them, and even when he found the words they were inadequate. He had a yearning for friendship, yet was awkward and prickly in the practice of it. He wore out welcomes very quickly, never quite understanding why. There was a special innocence in his conviction that truth, like the philosopher's stone, had a virtue of its own which would transmute dross into gold and put an end to all argument. He loved women and women were attracted to him, until they discovered that he was as much in love with knowing as he was with them, that, even after the ecstasies of the bed, he would still be reaching out for star fire in the distant skies. They thought him inconstant—yet constancy in a family was his unspoken need. He had, however, a greater need for the liberty he had not begun to experience, a liberty of the spirit to imagine even impossibles, to be a fabulist of that most fabulous of mysteries, Creation itself.

After the long darkness of the Middle Ages, in the face of all the bloody confusions of our own time, all of us looked backwards to a golden age of art, of letters, of law and of human conduct. We knew it had existed, because of the fragments which remained to us, more and more of which were being restored to us by Greek, Arabic and Jewish scholars and the patronage of enlightened princes like Cosimo di Medici. We believed that the restoration could be completed by a kind of magical rebirth. Even the Church, fractured and fragmented by doctrinal and dynastic disputes, could be restored by a return to its origins, the good news preached by Jesus on the lake shore of Galilee.

After the sterile dialectic of my monastic schooling in Naples, I was open to this hopeful dreaming. I read avidly whatever texts I could find: Lactantius on the writings of the ancient sage Hermes Trismegistus; the texts themselves, the *Corpus Hermericum* and the *Asclepius*, translated by Ficino at the express order of Cosimo di Medici. He rated this task more important than Ficino's translation of Plato.

For many scholars of our time—and we are still in our time, though I shall soon be out of it!—these writings contained the key to all knowledge, the pristine theology, the primal source of ancient wisdom, an historic magic that could change the world, as it had changed it for the ancients.

What was more natural, therefore, than when I began to write, to set down my system of memory and my visions of a new age, I should use not merely the literary conventions of dialogues and disputes between ancient gods, but the vocabularies of astrology, divination and occult knowledge. There was, in my opinion, nothing presumptuous or heretical in this. Saint Augustine and Lactantius both agreed that Hermes had discovered much truth and had affirmed the excellence and the majesty of the *Logos,* the Divine word.

The Church—especially the Roman Church—has its own language, and its own formulae of magic. The priest says "This is my body" and bread is changed into the flesh of Christ by a mystical process called transubstantiation. The priest says "I absolve you from your sins in the name of the Father, the Son and the Holy

Spirit". Immediately the soul—which is whatever it is—is cleansed of all iniquity, providing—there is sometimes a proviso, sometimes not—that the penitent is disposed to repentance and change. Baptism, on the other hand, is pure magic—a newborn babe, an inheritor of the guilt of Adam and Eve, is transmuted into a child of Christ, heir to the kingdom of heaven.

So you see, when I used the Hermetic language, I thought I was on solid ground supported by good authorities, enough at least to give credit to my arguments. I still think so, but for more than seven years now I have been engaged in a dialogue of the deaf with the Inquisitors—which is just about as useful as butting my head against the bastions of the Pope's own fortress, Castel Sant'Angelo.

The Inquisitors affirm the charges of heresy; I deny them. I write explanations that nobody reads. I send petitions to the Pope. He does not read them either. I do not expect him or them to believe me. I say only that I have the right to walk my own path in search of truth. They will not have that. I must believe what they tell me to believe. I must confess it in the terms they dictate. If I refuse, they will kill me.

This is the feast day of Saint Stephen, the first martyr of Christendom, stoned for heresy by the orthodox of his time while Saul of Tarsus, the zealous prosecutor, held the cloaks of the executioners. Later, Saul was converted by a miracle on the road to Damascus. I wonder if any miracle will change the minds of the Inquisitors and of His Holiness the Pope.

I can think no further forward than this, so I turn backward to my first journey into France: over the Alps to Chambéry in the Savoy.

I remember Chambéry as a small, industrious, beautiful town, where I was received courteously. However, there was no work for me here, so I was forced, once again, to turn for hospitality to the local community of my Order. This involved another change of dress and another series of fictions to explain my presence. I am not proud of these episodes; I plead only that they were a stratagem of survival.

Soon I was on the road again, this time to Geneva, where a

Neapolitan gentleman, the Marchese de Vico, was known to extend hospitality and support to Italians who adhered to the Protestant faith of the Calvinists.

De Vico received me warmly. He presented me with new clothes befitting a scholar and explained I could live in Geneva in peace and security, provided I showed a decent respect for the religion and the laws of the city. He explained the Genevan system of government by councils and the close cooperation of these councils with the religious consistory set up by John Calvin. I confess I listened with less attention than the situation demanded. Like a true Neapolitan, I was born to the conviction that most things could be settled 'by arrangement'.

De Vico, for example, told me it was not necessary to become a formal member of the Calvinist community, though I could attend services and even receive the sacrament. Following his advice, I signed my name in the Rector's Book at the university, attended lectures and joined in the debates. One of the professors was a certain Antoine de la Faye, a philosopher, a biblical scholar and, more importantly, a friend of the Rector. I was less than impressed by what I heard in his sessions. I noted twenty errors in a single lecture. These I caused to be published by a local printer. Immediately both the printer and I were arrested for uttering a libel. The printer blamed me and got a small fine. I insisted on pleading my cause and defending my arguments. I was imprisoned for my pains. Once again, I had misread the signs of the times and the tolerances of the godly.

I appealed to the Consistory. I apologised for my intemperate attack on the scholar. Clemency was granted. I was set free, but it was suggested very formally that I would be happier and safer elsewhere. Since it was only twenty-three years since they had burned Michael Servetus for heresy I had to agree.

I left Geneva in a hurry and headed west to Toulouse. I did not know—how could I?—that twenty years later the events in Geneva would be alleged against me by the Venetian and Roman Inquisitors.

Now, too late, I am convinced of the folly of entering into

dispute with any State or established religion. New ideas are a threat to stability. Therefore, they must be suppressed. Error has no right to exist. Those who propagate it must be destroyed. No argument in the world can prevail against the exercise of naked power.

So why do I go on trying? What do I expect from this solitary, surreptitious labour in my cell? The question was put to me many times by different people. All of them asked: "Why do you fight? Why not give them what they want: recantation, submission, a show of wise obedience? It's a formality they need. Let them have it. Afterwards you can go back in peace to your monastery garden and still believe what you choose."

But then I have questions of my own. What will be left of me to live with in my convent garden? Whom shall I see when I look into a mirror? A cherub with a vacant smile and not a brain left in his empty head? How can I endure that? How can I forgive myself the lies that I should have to tell to bring me to this happy state?

Oh, I have told lies before! I have hidden uncomfortable truths, as once, all those years ago, I hid Master Erasmus's works in the privy in San Domenico. I can live with those defaults, even hope to be forgiven them, because I acknowledge them for what they are: the tricks of a harried fox to put the hounds off scent.

But there are happier times to remember. My sojourn in Toulouse, the ancient capital of Languedoc, is one of them. After the massacre of Saint Bartholomew's Day in Paris, there were attacks on Protestant communities up and down the kingdom. However, by the time I arrived in Toulouse, the city was relatively calm. I took lodgings in the house of Berthe Maupin, widow of an advocate, a comely and comfortable woman to whom I had been recommended by a gentleman with whom I travelled from Lyons. It was this same gentleman who gave me the good news that teachers at the university were elected by students and no public profession of faith or participation in the sacrament was demanded.

I began, as I had done elsewhere, by assembling a small group of interested students with whom I worked privately. Then, as my reputation grew—and it grew very fast—I asked to be examined for the degree of Master of Theology. My degree once conferred, I applied for a lectureship, to which I was immediately elected.

I still have a pride in that appointment. I came to it on merit, without patronage. I gave, I believe, good value for my stipend. I taught two courses: one Aristotle's *de Anima,* and the other on the Art of Memory. Each of these courses I made into a book, which earned me some extra money and certainly added to my reputation as a philosopher.

I made no enemies that I can remember in Toulouse. My lectures attracted many students. My feats of memory amazed them. Among my peers I made a small group of friends, some of whom were serviceable to me later in Paris. The widow Maupin was kind to me and I like to think I was kind to her. She had a comfortable inheritance from her husband, and she had neither need or expectation of wealth from a non-tenured scholar. I was younger and lustier than the man she had lost. She fed me well and kept my linen clean and my hose darned. We served each other well in bed. We lived quietly and discreetly while I worked on my lectures and my books. I smile as I remember how regular, and indeed almost conventual our domestic existence was.

I ask myself also how my life might have turned out if I had invested it in a career at this provincial university. Marriage would have presented a problem, of course. Berthe was a Catholic—and I was a renegade priest and a monk still under solemn vows from which only the Pope could dispense me. So on all counts, discreet concubinage was the best estate for us both. We could have continued in it placidly for many years. Berthe was willing. I was the fellow with the imp of ambition whispering always in his ear, urging him *ad altiora:* to higher and greater things.

To rise higher I needed a thrust which the Chancellor and faculty of Toulouse could not give me. First I had to go to Paris. To establish myself there, I needed to present myself as an original and challenging philosopher.

So, as part of my preparation, I devised a series of lectures on the Divine Attributes as treated by Aquinas. These I would advertise in the city with the help of a printer to make and distribute notices. There is always an audience in every city for conjurers and jugglers and clever soothsayers.

The lectures would establish my orthodoxy, in a capital where orthodoxy had been confirmed by bloodshed. At the same time, I would prepare the outline of a work on natural magic and a system of memory, of which I myself am a skilled exponent and example. I can claim to have in effect the memory of a magus who, through the ancient images which he has learned and understood, has achieved an enormous personal power. I hoped that my exposition of that power might bring me to the attention of the court and indeed to the King himself, who, according to rumour, was devoted to liberal arts but lived, uneasy and afraid, with the ghosts of his recent past.

My Berthe knew nothing and cared nothing about philosophy, but she did understand my need to advance myself. We did not quarrel over my decision. We wept together and Berthe warned me gently: "It's easy, my love, to take the eggs from your own hens, but eagles make their nests in high and dangerous places and they are hostile birds. So take care, my love. I shall miss you. Will you write to me sometimes?"

I promised I would, but I never did. This is the curse of the vagabond: he can never look back. No matter how comfortable the bed he has shared, he is always solitary on the road.

27 December

Today I am a prey to winter gloom: a suffocating melancholy which, if I yield to it, will leave me lying on my bed staring at the grey stones of the ceiling. I have to force myself to wash, cram down the stale bread of my breakfast, and settle myself to write. The cloud of sadness lifts as I call up my memories of my first stay in Paris, which are among the happiest of my life.

I had prepared myself well for this sojourn. I was tired of the footloose life of a vagabond scholar. My time with Berthe had taught me the value of domestic tranquillity. I had spent sparingly in Toulouse, so I had a modest amount of money in my purse, enough to buy myself a saddle horse, and pay the expenses on the road and of living, while I sought a patronage in Paris.

I had letters of introduction from a colleague to three printers in Paris and to two members of the faculty at the Sorbonne, where my colleague had studied. In short, I was in better case than I had ever been on my wanderings, but I knew I had to start work as soon as possible.

By a happy chance, all the printers to whom I had letters were in the Rue Saint Jean de Latran quite near the College of Cambrai. One was Egidius Gilles at the sign of the Three Crowns, the second Egidius Gorbin, whose signboard announced 'Hope', and Guillame Giuliano who was a nephew of Gorbin.

I decided to split my work among the three, which would put them in competition with each other, and stretch my credit a little further. Every printer needs authors to keep his presses busy and give him stock to sell to booksellers and at fairs. The printers were eager to present me to their clients as a new and distinguished figure on their lists, so I was invited to speak at various gatherings of scholars and nobles. More quickly than I had dared to hope, a conduit was opened between me and the court of King Henry III.

The Venetian envoy, Giovanni Moro, lent me most generous support and taught me the ways of courtly life. My dear and devoted friend, Jean Regnault, presented me to Henry of Angouleme, Grand Prior of the Realm, Lieutenant General and Admiral of the Fleet. To these nobles and others like them, I was able to demonstrate in detail my system of memory, a great improvement on that devised by Raymond Lull.

I asked them to test me, both on commitment and recall, in subjects of their choice: history, geography, astronomy and the mythologies of the ancients. I confess that in all my performances I used little mystifying tricks like a performer in a masque or a conjuror in a carnival. There is a child in all of us who delights in illusion.

I did not discourage gossip and debate on whether the art I demonstrated was natural or magical, though I was careful not to assert—other than by rhetorical exaggeration—that it did contain elements of ancient magic. In the atmosphere of discussion and suspicion created by the religious wars, the last thing I needed was another allegation of heresy!

Finally, I received a royal summons to appear at court, to demonstrate my system. As part of my exposition, I pointed out that a man with a well-trained memory was the safest courier for high messages. There were no documents that could be stolen or copied. All the messenger needed was a mark of identity. In a certain sense he would be proof even against torture, since the infliction of pain would confuse the carefully contrived symbols of recall. This I admit was an untested assertion, but at the time it seemed a reasonable idea.

His Majesty then submitted me to a test of his own devising. He had caused to be prepared a document of some length containing diplomatic and military instructions on a fictitious operation in Flanders. He asked how much time I needed to commit it to memory. I asked for five minutes, but after three minutes of reading I rolled up the parchment and handed it back. I then recited it back word for word, and asked to be tested on detail by random questions from His Majesty and others.

In my present lowly estate, I still remember that as a triumphant occasion. The confidence of my noble friends was vindicated. His Majesty was vastly impressed. He ordered that a teaching post be found for me at the College de France, and told me in clear terms that he would consider what other uses might be found for my singular skills.

Within a very short time, I had completed three works, all rooted in the mnemonic art: *Architecture in the Books of Raymond Lull*, *The Shadows of Ideas* and *Circe's Song*. Looking back at them now, I recognise that they were more important to my career than to posterity. Even then I wanted to escape from this somewhat sterile corner of the garden of philosophy. It was, in its day, a phenomenon, but it signified little in real progress to wisdom and enlightenment. I felt the need of a change from pedantry to the comedy of real life. I turned my mind back to other masters—Bibbiena, Ariosto, Aretino and decided that I had experience and literary skill to match them. I wrote a play! It was a comedy which I called *The Candle Maker*.

As I sit, cold and solitary in my cell, looking at my own meagre supply of candles, I recall how boldly I presented my prologue to *The Candle Maker*.

"You must imagine yourselves in the Most Royal City of Naples… You will catch glimpses of cheats, rogues and cutpurses… virile women, effeminate men… You will see little of beauty, nothing of good… Heaven help you!"

As a satire on the life of monks and the careers of pedants, it was, as they say, drawn from life. As a piece of theatre, it was successful and talked of all over Paris. As an episode in my chequered career, it was, in retrospect, ill omened. It made me as many enemies as friends, and it was used against me from the beginning of my trials in Venice and in Rome.

Let me admit that my life in Paris gave me much pleasure but no more faith in the goodness of human beings. I had my post at the College de France because that was the King's gift, but the Sorbonne was closed to me because there the Church was triumphant, and desperate to defend herself against the encroachment of suspected heretics like me. The success of my comedy increased the threat. Dubious theology is one thing. You can debate it or suppress it. Popular satire is quite another matter. You can never stifle the mocking laughter in the crowd, so you set the hounds on the man who provoked it.

For the moment, however, their baying was hardly audible behind the applause of my admirers and the eager responses of the students who crowded into my lectures. I had made it clear from the beginning that they were free to put any question they chose, and frame it even in the most contentious terms.

"A scholar," I told them, "a true scholar, is one in love with knowing. He must be willing to sell the last shirt off his back for one small truth, one hint of star fire to light up the mystery of this world and all that lies beyond it. To make definitions and compose formulae is not knowledge. That is pedantry and I will not have it from you in this room. Language, my friends, is the most seductive and the most treacherous of gifts, because all languages are constructed by men and women. It is only the capacity to construct them which we can claim to have from the Creator. Ever since the Greeks, we have been drunk with eloquence. We have made a cage of words and shoved the Creator inside, as boys confine a cricket or a locust to make him sing a private song! But once the singer is imprisoned there is no song anymore, there is the silence of a god dying in a narrow dark room…"

They understood that. At least I believed they did. I read it in their eyes. I heard it in their exhalations of surprise and wonder, which lifted me to flights of bolder speculation. This was the freedom I had always craved: to speak my mind and have others respond in approval or rebuttal. I did not care either way, just so they did not sit like empty vessels waiting dumbly for some scholastic cellarmaster to fill them with thin wine already on the turn to vinegar.

I was careful, however, to make a reserve of time for more private studies. I sought out those who were—or claimed to be—adepts in the practice of alchemy, which deals with the transformations that can be affected within matter itself: how, for example, base metals can be transformed into gold or silver. There is much nonsense talked and written about this secret art. Many who claim to practise it are the basest of charlatans.

However, I did meet one authentic character. His name was Don Miguel Maravilloso, who gave himself out as a Spaniard but was more probably of an old Morisco family which had converted from Islam in earlier times and then fled the country into exile.

This Maravilloso was a tall, swarthy fellow in his early sixties, with a smile that came rarely and eyes that read the secrets behind the faces of other men. He had made a high reputation and a good living as an armourer, selling fine swords and daggers to noblemen at the fencing school which he had founded. His weapons of damascened steel were highly prized among the nobility whom he schooled.

I could not afford his wares, but I was able to engage his interest by my knowledge of Hermetic crafts, of which the forging of metal is the most ancient and most mysterious. He opened himself to me cautiously at first and then with the freedom of a friend. I recall as if it were yesterday our most revealing talk.

"...I learned my skills from my father, he from his father and so on, backward into a dim past which goes back to Alexandria and Carthage. They taught me more than the craft, they taught me the magic that infuses it, and the language that expresses it."

"When you say magic, Don Miguel, what do you mean? Good magic, bad magic, spells, incantations?"

He laughed and shook his head.

"No, Master Giordano! No and no again! What I call magic is not what I do but what happens when I do it."

"You will have to explain that."

"You know how fine steel is tempered, firstly by heating it and then plunging it into water?"

"I know it as a fact, but that is all. I can neither do it nor explain it."

"There, you have it exactly! I am a master swordsmith—better than most in this city. A lesser man can do what I do, use the same elements and produce a blade that is no better than a butcher's cleaver. What makes me different? What is it in my inheritance which endows me with a master's judgement? That's the magic! All the rest is ritual. Name me the four elements."

"Earth, air, fire and water."

"Exactly. I use them all in my smithing—the metal dug from the earth, the air in my bellows, the fire in my furnace, the water in my barrel. But what happens inside the blade I make? I don't know. I cry to know, but one day, in some magical moment, the knowing will come to someone. Think! The ancients claimed that the art of working metal was learned from Vulcan toiling with the cyclops at his forge in the bottom of the volcano of Etna. That's legend. The mystery is who taught men that instead of stone axes they could make bronze ones. Who taught them how to make iron and forge steel? Who taught them to fuse sand into glass? I believe that all such knowledge comes in moments of inspired guess-work. Those who make the guesses are the true magicians. We craftsmen are the adepts who inherit their secrets. We keep the knowledge to ourselves, we hide it in a babble of incantations, because we know it gives us power. Now, Master Giordano, do you think you can explain that to your students? Do you dare to proclaim it in your writing?"

"Is that a challenge, my friend?"

"A caution perhaps. I make a fine rapier, which can kill a man or with which I myself can be killed. So I make a scabbard to shield the blade and myself. These are dangerous times. What you teach, what you write, are weapons that can be turned against you."

"So a careful language is the scabbard in which I hide then?"

"Until you are angry enough or bold enough or foolish enough to unsheathe the blade, strip the rhetoric away and tell the naked truth. That's the first lesson I teach my students. Never invite combat. Never threaten another man unless you are prepared to kill him or be killed yourself."

"Why are you so concerned for me?"

"Why do I talk to you at all?" He laughed again. "Perhaps because you are a man with shadows in his past, as I am. That, at least, is the gossip I hear. I hear, too, that you dream and talk of a new future. I do the same when I am happy in my laboratory. I ask myself what secrets we may learn from tomorrow. I wonder what travellers may bring back from far places—like Cathay and the New Indies. The problem is that our futures may threaten others who are mortally afraid of change."

"How else can change be made if we do not contrive it?"

"As I forge my steel: in private, and only for those who value it."

It was after this conversation that I asked whether I might visit him at his forge and in his laboratory. He smiled and shook his head.

"You would learn nothing, Master Giordano. A forge is a forge, a blacksmith is a blacksmith. As for my laboratory, all you would get would be a headache from the vapours, stains on your hands and your clothes from the liquors. I could make stinks and explosions for you and distil a coloured liquor in my alembic. But these would be conjurer's tricks. They do not answer the real questions: what makes the steel change colour, why will some metals combine with each other, what is the difference between a living tree and the charcoal which derives from it? You and I walk different roads to the same truth. Who knows but that I may one day prove in my laboratory what you conjecture in some magical night of silence? But be careful, Master Giordano. Think well! This is the age of madness. We burn maidens and grandmothers for witchcraft. What may they do with us when they discover how little we know?"

I did not hear and I did not heed the warning. I was flying too high, a falcon riding the wind.

I was much at court. His Majesty was at ease in the company of scholars and philosophers, with whom he would spend two and three hours a day in readings and discussions. He appointed me as one of his Readers, a position which raised some jealousies, but also put money in my pocket. More than this, I was for a while quite desperately in love.

Egidius Gorbin, the printer in whose house I lodged, was a man of singular charity. He had devoted time and money to the care of those children of members of the Printers' Guild who had been orphaned by the death of both parents or left destitute by the loss of the breadwinner. He found foster parents for them and, as they grew older, he placed the boys in apprenticeships, and had the girls trained in such domestic arts as might qualify them to make a reasonable marriage within the ranks of the guild.

The girls were schooled in the house of Mademoiselle Françoise Solanges. One evening, over a glass of wine, Egidius Gorbin asked a small favour: would I be willing to visit Mademoiselle Solanges and talk to her young ladies? I was not too happy with the idea. I felt I had served my term as an ill-paid dominie and I had no experience at all with a classroom full of young girls. Gorbin insisted in his quiet fashion. He would like to oblige the lady. I might be interested in the special quality of care she gave to her charges. In any case, it would be a change from the disputes of the lecture hall and the intrigues of the court. I could find no good reason to refuse, so, early one morning, I presented myself at the house of Françoise Solanges, a discreet dwelling in one of the lanes behind the College de France.

Even in the squalor and despair of my present situation, I discover a lively joy in the memory of that first encounter with Françoise Solanges. I was stunned by her physical beauty: auburn hair, green eyes, a skin like the whitest marble and a figure, hidden, but somehow the more openly displayed by the sober gown and her stomacher of peasant lace. Her smile, like her greeting, was candid and open—a pleasant change from the coquetries and the bitcheries of the ladies of the court. To my entranced eyes, she seemed bathed in calm, like the moonlight on lake water. Yet I felt a sudden prickling of lust for her, a lust I dared not reveal so soon but which, like every hopeful lecher, I dreamed one day to confess.

The pupils ranged from twelve to five years. It was obvious that they adored her. They treated her like an older sister, eager for her notice and the comfort of her presence and her touch. There was nothing niggard in the affection she lavished on them. I prayed silently that she might spend a little on me.

I asked her what she thought I had to offer to her girls. Her answer surprised me.

"I want you to set them dreaming. I am told this is what you have done for your students both in Toulouse and Paris. I want you to open a garden in which my girls can walk for the rest of their lives."

"And what makes you think I can do that, Mademoiselle?"

"Egidius Gorbin assures me that you can. He talks of your prodigious powers of memory. Gossip says you are an adept in black arts."

"Do you believe that?"

"No. I believe Monsieur Gorbin. He calls you a cloud-walker. Now that I've met you, I think it's a good name. I'd like you to take my girls for a walk in the clouds, show them the blue that lies beyond them and the stars that lie beyond the blue."

"Is that important to young ladies?"

"It's important to all of us, Master Bruno. Women, no less than men, need a future in which to vest their hopes."

"I should have thought their hopes were built on marriage and children."

She laughed at that, and as I write I remember that her laugh was like the sound of silver bells. Our first moment of intimacy ended there. She led me into the salon where her girls were waiting, wide eyed, whispering and giggling at the short, swarthy fellow in the scholar's gown, who, for the first time in his life, was tongue-tied with women. Then suddenly, as with the mute man in the Gospel, the string of my tongue was loosened and I began to tell them the story of my own childhood in Nola, of the woods and groves of Mount Cicada and the mythical creatures who dwelt there, nymphs and satyrs and centaurs and Pan who played the pipes and Apollo who made music on his lyre. Then I invited them to ride with me, on a great puff of smoke from Vesuvius, and stride over the clouds into an infinity of stars and undiscovered earths.

I did not talk down to them from a rostrum but moved among them, kneeling sometimes, squatting on the floor and drawing them into a circle around me, sometimes mincing like an actor in a *commedia dell'arte*. I was surrounded by their fresh womanhood—a faun in a field of asphodels but a child, too, reliving innocent hours among his playmates. I know that I was happy that day. I know the children were, and afterwards, in the privacy of her parlour, Françoise Solanges held my hands for a moment in her own and told me: "You had me walking the clouds with you, Master Bruno. I cannot thank you enough for coming."

"I should like to come again."

"I hope you will, as often as you are disposed."

"And for my part, Mademoiselle, I would hope we may sometimes walk out together—just you and I in a private cloudland."

She gave me a strange wry smile and shook her head. "I think that would not be a good idea."

"Why not? Are you betrothed? Are you afraid of scandal?"

"Neither!"

"I displease you then?"

"On the contrary, I am honoured that you ask me."

"So, what is the problem?"

"The problem, dear Master Bruno, is that there is no place in my life for a man, even one so attractive as you. There's a place for friendship—even a friendship of the heart—but for more than that, no. My life is complete in itself. I spend my womanhood on my girls, to make them finally into women. In return they lend me their youth and their love."

"And that is enough? For ever and a day?"

"When it ceases to be enough, there is another step for me to take."

"And what is that?"

"When we know each other a little better, Master Bruno—and I confess my hope that we shall—then I shall tell you."

And with that, perforce, I had to be content, but in the days and weeks that followed I was plagued by desire for this woman, harried by furies of jealousy and suspicion. Yet I dared not risk a word or a gesture that might alienate her from me.

Twice a week at least I visited her house. I played memory games with the girls, read them legends and poetry, schooled them in the elementary rules of rhetoric. Their aptitude and enthusiasm opened my monkish eyes to the talents of women—too little regarded in our male world. It also rewarded me with a sense of familial attachment long absent from my vagabond life.

At the end of each session, I drank a glass of wine and talked in private with Françoise. My passion for her grew stronger, but she offered to me no more than a calm, sisterly affection which left me still excluded and frustrated. Came a day when I could contain myself no longer. I sat beside her, imprisoned her hands in mine and poured out my love and my longing in a rush of ardent words.

She did not withdraw from me; she did not yield either. There were tears in her eyes, but she sat still and calm, as if gathering herself to damn me for my folly. Instead, she admonished me with singular gentleness.

"My dear friend—and you are, believe me, my dear, dear friend—I told you from the beginning that there is no place for a man in my life. I am not like other women. My needs and my gifts, too, are different."

"How different? Tell me, please! Help me to understand."

"If I tell you that, dear Master Bruno, I am putting my life in your hands."

"I have already put my heart in yours."

She shook her head, in despair at my lack of understanding. Then she lifted up her arms to unclasp from her neck a silver chain from which a pendant hung, invisible between her breasts. She did not show me the pendant immediately, but held it for a moment concealed in her clenched hand, hesitating to display it. Finally, she opened her palm and offered me the object: a circle of antique gold, with a boss in the centre like the boss on a shield and, radiating from the centre, four spokes, like the spokes of a wheel, except that they were not spaced evenly. One pair was widely spread, the other enclosed a narrower segment of circle.

I knew instantly what it was. I had seen it illustrated in documents of my Order of Friars Preachers dating back to the thirteenth century. I had been lectured on their cultic meaning. I had been shown similar objects as curiosities during my recent sojourn in Toulouse: a coin, a medallion, a curious cross with a bird perched on it.

They were the symbols of the Cathar sect, once the prevailing faith all over Languedoc, before its adherents were massacred as heretics in a series of military crusades launched by Pope Innocent III. After that, they were harassed into near extinction by Inquisitors from my own Order. Their doctrines, declared heretical and destructive of social order, were derived from ancient Manichean teachings that the world was a battleground between two conflicting deities, the Maker of Good and the Maker of Evil, spirit on the one hand, matter on the other. In spite of the sanctity of many of its believers, it was regarded as a false and pernicious doctrine to be extirpated wherever it appeared.

I was amazed that Françoise should have trusted me so far. Even in those days in France, three centuries later, the mere possession of the talisman might have laid her open to indictment on charges of heresy and treason. The massacre of the Huguenots on Saint Bartholomew's Eve was still a recent memory, and the religious wars were far from over.

Françoise was watching me, waiting for my response. I found myself stammering over the simple question: what did the symbol mean to her? She answered calmly.

"It means that I am a Cathar. My family came from Albi, which was from earliest times a city of our people. We had our own clergy, our own rites, even our own coinage. Many of the noblest families in Languedoc were believers. Our traditions go back many centuries to the wise men of Persia, who believed in the eternal opposition between good and evil, spirit and matter."

She broke off, smiling, and reached out to touch my hand.

"But why am I instructing you? You know all this. The friars of your Order followed the armies to convert those of my people who had escaped the massacres. My family was one of those which survived and handed down our traditions from each generation to the next. When my mother died, I promised her that one day I would take the sacrament which we call the 'Consolation'. Once you take it, you join the ranks of 'The Perfect Ones' who renounce marriage and all carnal intercourse to live the life of the spirit. For obvious reasons, most of our people chose to defer the act until late in life so that they could live normally like their neighbours, and even seem to identify with them—as I do here."

I was about to ask why she had chosen so early in life to accept the ascetic discipline of The Perfect Ones, but she forestalled me.

"You must know, dear friend, that I have always been happier in the company of women than among the menfolk. Even as a child, when I heard the tales that were told of the bad old days, I used to have nightmares in which I was impaled on the lance or the sword of a man in armour. Living as I live now, I have no nightmares. I am like the eldest in a family of loving sisters. The youngest ones are like my own children. I do not feel deprived but enriched. I am not cold. I am not incapable of love. Indeed, dear Master Bruno, I can say truthfully that I love you; but I cannot offer you what other women can. I do not despise it. It is simply that I cannot return it as you would like."

Suddenly, all my anger was spent and I found myself weeping quietly. She came and knelt beside me, holding me protectively, comforting me like a child.

"Please, please, dear brother. Don't cry. Don't you understand what I have told you? What I have shown you is proof that I love you. You hold my life and my happiness in your hands. Forgive me for what I cannot give you."

There was nothing to forgive. I told her that. She had not shamed me, as some women can shame a man by rejection or ridicule. She had dignified me beyond all my deserts. I begged her to forgive my intrusion into her secret life and to understand that, in her special circumstances, I could be a risk to her, because I, too, was a man at risk. Before I left, we kissed for the first and the last time, yet her presence in my life is still important enough to record in this document, which may well turn out to be my obituary.

Her steadfastness in her own beliefs gave me courage to hold to mine. She taught me that the right to believe is more important than the belief itself, that the liberty to be mistaken is the liberty most difficult to defend. Through her, I understood that the last keep in the last fortress is that in which our identity, our only self, resides. To surrender that is to incur the ultimate damnation: nothingness. This is the surrender which they will demand of me very soon. I look to her to strengthen me in the testing time.

I kept her secret as I promised. Her life depended on it. My own tattered honour was pledged to it. I am absolved from my promise now, because Françoise Solanges is dead these many years, victim of a plague which struck Paris just after my departure for England. Egidius Gorbin sent me the news by a letter in care of my host, the French Ambassador in London. I offered a private Mass in his house for the repose of the sweet soul of Françoise Solanges.

As I remember that requiem, it is as if she sits with me in my cell, a figure out of the mists of history like Sappho among her women on Lesbos. I ask myself how God could judge her otherwise than gently, and how He will judge my so righteous accusers who claim that error has no right to exist, and that it is better to burn men than permit them to breathe one small vapour of error into the air.

It is late. I must remember to save my candle. Enough of memory, sad or sweet. I am desperate for sleep.

29 December

I wrote nothing yesterday. I spent all day curled on my bed, courting sleep but lapsing only into nightmares, from which I woke choking on my own tongue as if I had died, and gone to hell and then been brutally resurrected.

The project I had undertaken, to write a commentary on my yesterdays, seemed an exercise in futility. Who would read the pages, once the ashes of their author were scattered to the winds? Who would hear the piping of a pale ghost in an empty square at midnight? And where would I be, Filippo Giordano Bruno, called the Nolan, despatched by decree out of this life into another?

It was the thought of that other world which reduced me to destructive lethargy. That I should enter it soon was certain. But in what mode or form? To what new motion or progression? Towards what end? Or in what ceaseless traverse of infinity? And who or what Divinity would determine the outcomes?

Holy Mother Church, in which I had spent my life, had taught me that the moment of death was a moment of private judgement and accounting between creature and Creator. It taught more, that she herself was the sole authentic mediator at this judgement seat, that she alone, in the person of her Pontiff, possessed the fullness of power even up to the threshold of the afterlife.

Therefore, according to this reasoning, if she casts me out I am left without friend or advocate at the judgement seat of the Almighty. The ritual words of formal excommunication have been familiar to me since my earliest days in the Order which, I keep reminding myself, has had for centuries a remit from the Holy See to purge out the unorthodox:

> We declare you to be an impenitent heretic, and therefore to have incurred all the ecclesiastical censures and pains of the Holy Canon, the laws and the constitutions, both general and particular... And we hereby ordain and command that you shall be actually degraded from all your ecclesiastical orders, both major and minor, in which you have been ordained, according to the Sacred Canon Law; and that you must be driven forth, and we do drive you forth from our ecclesiastical forum and from our Holy and Immaculate Church of whose mercy you have become unworthy.

It is a monstrous proposition, from which all belief abdicates, against which reason itself revolts and the human heart hardens into absolute rejection. I cannot believe that the Creator treats with His own handiwork as the Inquisitors treat with me in His name. The faces which stare at me from their rostrum are masks devoid of all humanity, their eyes are empty of pity. I am the scapegoat, loaded with their sins, whom they will drive out into the desert to perish, while they rejoice in their own righteousness.

Sometimes, on black days like this, I have contemplated suicide. It would not be too hard to open a vein in my wrist at bedtime and sleep my way into peace. Alternately, I could take the way which the Cathars call *endura* and starve myself to death. I fear, however, that I have left this solution too late. I could fast for forty days and still survive to be burnt.

This is the fish bone that sticks in my gullet. For murder or rape, you execute a man. So be it! Eye for eye, tooth for tooth. But for an idea? An intangible? An opinion held in private or uttered in public? The option is intolerable: profess as we do or be for ever mute!

What I want to say, in this my last testament, is that I know what I am, what I have been and what I am believed to be: failed priest, fugitive monk, magus with a box of conjuring tricks, boaster, prevaricator, would-be torchbearer trudging through his own darkness, garrulous in dialogue, viperous in debate. All of this. More if you can find the words!

Yet there is something else. I have known many women and loved all too few, but I am in love with knowing and with truth. God knows, I pray little, but there is one prayer I do make: give me light, give me eyes to see it, give me courage to testify to the vision. Amen.

And on that 'amen' my long blank day ended. I lapsed into a sleep of exhaustion and woke renewed to continue this testimony.

In France, I had been at first happy and busy. My lectures were well attended. I attracted students and disciples. I wrote steadily, four works in Latin on various aspects of the Art of Memory: *Ars memoriae, De umbris idearum, Cantus circaeus, De compendiosa architectura et complemento artis Lullii.* In addition to these, I produced my most successful comedic work, this time in Italian: *Il Candelaio.*

All this represented a respectable body of work. The reputation it earned for me was well deserved. It gave the lie to later accusations that I was a dissolute vagabond, a cleric bent only on lechery. In all truth, I had not the time nor the energy for such a life.

I was what I had always wanted to be: a scholar, a respected philosopher, publicly acclaimed for his works. I went regularly to court, in my capacity as Royal Lector. I enjoyed the gracious favours of His Majesty. I had my private friendships among the nobles of his entourage, as well as among the scholars and the printers. I had women friends who received me readily, and there was always my strange frustrating attachment to Françoise Solanges.

That was, if you like to call it so, one panel of the diptych. The other was dark and turbulent. Catholics and Protestants (in France called Huguenots) were in a state of sporadic war. The King, for all his graciousness to me—and let me say it plain: my fulsome diplomatic praise of him—was never in full control of the situation. There were riots and tumults in Paris and other cities. There were affrays in the university itself, which reminded me of my student days in Naples. There were also individual acts of violence, vendettas which dated back ten years to the first massacres. There were assassins at large in the cities, hired to settle old scores.

There was danger for me, too. I had rivals and enemies. I was, after all, a foreigner, a man with a cloud over his character, a contentious scholar, impatient of fools and pedants, lacking the discretion to lead a quiet life in a complicated situation. Eddies and currents formed about me as they would about a tree branch, fallen and stuck midstream in a swift river.

There were many reasons, and I myself was not the least of them. There were angers in me which I had scarcely begun to recognise, let alone to master. My own ambition for fame—and my need to establish a standing place in my insecure existence—made me assertive and often indiscreet. I had been educated in absolutes—legal, theological, philosophic. When my convictions changed, as they did, I still remained an absolutist in temper. I defended my own hilltop against all comers, even though quiet discussion and some compromise might have enabled me to possess the same ground in peace and security.

For a time, I was able to live within my private world, ignore the rising gales outside, and delude myself—an illusion fostered by monastic training—that I belonged to a privileged caste amenable only to its own code and its own courts. The fact that I had attempted to place myself outside their community was in a sense irrelevant. Their authorities reasoned that I was still bound and could be reclaimed by law. So even my interior life was subject to currents of unease, while my friends continued their gentle persuasion that I should move on, preferably to the domain of a Protestant prince where, in theory at least, my aberrant philosophy would not be construed as a threat to public order.

At face value, it was sound advice; but in Geneva, for instance, I had found that Calvinists were just as intolerant as Catholics. However, there was a general agreement that, for one like myself, England offered the safest haven. It was an island kingdom. The Queen was head of Church and State. The writs of the Roman Inquisition did not run there. Foreigners with learning or craft skills, like the Flemish weavers, were welcomed. Queen Elizabeth was well disposed to Italians and even conversed in our language. The University of Oxford was in the first rank of institutions of learning. In the end, I decided that I had nothing to lose and perhaps much to gain across the Channel.

First, I begged leave of His Majesty, saying in jest that my departure would remove one pebble from his royal shoes, then suggesting that in England I might be able to offer him some service in return for his gracious favours to me. He liked that thought and promised that he would instruct me further. He granted me permission to leave his court and requested the British Ambassador, Sir Henry Cobham, to supply me with a *laisser-passer* into the realm of Queen Elizabeth. The Ambassador raised no objection, but made it clear that he had some reservations about my teaching and my papist faith, which, though I am often at odds with it, I cannot and will not deny. I am sure that he wrote in the same terms to his master in London, Sir Francis Walsingham, to inform him of my coming.

His Majesty then endowed me with the greatest mark of his favour: a letter of commendation to his own Ambassador in England, His Excellency Michel de Castelnau, Seigneur of Mauvissière, Concressault and Joinville. He made me a gift of money and assured me that, if ever I chose to return, I should be welcome in his kingdom.

I did not leave immediately, but made a round of calls on all my friends, and attended the dinner festivities they arranged in my honour. I also worked long and late to prepare a letter to the Vice-Chancellor at Oxford, begging him to receive me and to permit me to deliver an address to the faculty and scholars. I also set about preparing another work on memory for publication in England: *Triginta sigillorum explicatio*—an Explanation of the Thirty Seals. This was well-trodden ground for me, but I judged it might hold some surprises for the worthy doctors of Oxford.

Finally, after a last tender meeting with Françoise Solanges and her little family, I left Paris and rode to Calais, where I embarked for England. We made swift passage in a fair wind, and I still remember my excitement when the helmsman thrust out his arm and pointed to the cliffs of white chalk, the frontiers of this land, which had set itself beyond the reach of Rome and all her European allies. I remember my ironic thought that it might well be easier for me to be Catholic here than under the battlements of Castel Sant'Angelo in Rome.

It was April when I arrived. Spring was breaking out all over the countryside, so my progress to London was a compendium of pleasures for the eye and the spirit. I am a man of moods, sad and gay by unexpected turns. I felt isolated both by my studious pursuits and by my lack of knowledge of local speech. English is no easy language to understand. Taverns and post houses are not the best places to learn it. Nevertheless, I made an effort to engage in conversation any traveller who would talk to me.

There are many tribes and dialects among the English, just as there are in Italy. At first meeting, the English can be laconic and withdrawn, suspicious and patronising of the foreigner; but in their cups and in their friendships they can be open and warm. Their women, at least those whom I met, smiled readily, and were openly flirtatious with strangers like myself. I guessed that their lives were not always easy with the doughty country squires and hard-riding, hard-drinking young gentlemen to whom they were on offer or already traded in the marriage market.

In London, I was welcomed with overflowing generosity by the Ambassador, Michel de Castelnau. He was a handsome man in his early sixties with a winning smile and a talent for friendship rare in the duplicitous trade of diplomacy. He proposed that I should lodge in his house, and when I demurred, not wishing to put him about, he insisted.

"Master Bruno, this is the King's will and my pleasure. My wife offers you her welcome. My children will benefit from your instruction, my friends will be enriched by your company. I shall, myself, present you to Her Majesty and her ministers. She is well disposed to me, but her royal cousin, Mary, Queen of Scots, is god-mother to our daughter. My wife is related to her, and I am pledged to help her in any way I can. I make no secret of this, but I make no plots either, so the nobles of England are honoured to sit at my table. This country is probably the calmest place in Europe at this moment. Her Majesty is popular with the people. Even her Catholic subjects—most of them, at least—are loyal to the Crown and mis-trustful of Rome and of the Spaniards."

"And how will I be regarded by the scholars of England?"

He threw back his head and laughed heartily.

"How can I say, Master Bruno? I have been a soldier for half of my life and a courtier for the rest of it. I have many friends who are scholars, but I do not live in their world. My guess would be that the English are as jealous of their scholarship as they are of their island sovereignty. I am told you will speak at Oxford."

"If I am invited, yes."

"An invitation will be arranged. My Lord Leicester is the Chan-cellor. His nephew, Sir Philip Sidney, is a friend of mine. You shall meet him very soon. Now, let me introduce you to my people. Your countryman, John Florio, is tutor to my daughter."

I was happy in that household. I had a quiet room in which to work and I wrote prolifically and vigorously. When I needed fresh air, I could walk down Water Lane to the River Thames and watch the boat traffic and the flight of the gulls.

Castelnau introduced me at court. I was presented to Her Majesty, who was gracious to me and spoke with me in Italian. I met also her Chief Minister, Sir Francis Walsingham, who gave me a cor-dial greeting and then engaged me in a long conversation on my life, my experiences in Naples under the Spaniards, and my opinions on the religious wars in France. He was obviously impressed with what I told him and he made a discreetly veiled proposal that he would welcome a regular exchange of similar information. I told him, saving always my obligations in duty and friendship to my host, Castelnau,

I should be happy to oblige him. I saw at the time no conflict in this. I was a guest in his country, too. My continued sojourn depended on his favour and that of Her Majesty.

As it turned out, Oxford was a sour little episode in my English sojourn. The doctors and scholars were none too pleased when I challenged their obstinate attachment to Aristotle and suggested they consider the merits of other philosophers: Pythagoras, Parmenides, Anaxagoras. I made no secret of my shock to find that masters and scholars were fined five shillings for each and every error in their interpretations of Aristotle's *Organon* and that persistence in such errors would cause expulsion.

Even as I write these words, a bitter irony presents itself; a fine or even an expulsion were small penalties to pay for deviant opinions. Mine may well cost me my life!

There were other and more simple reasons for my failure to impress the worthy dons of Oxford. I was most obviously a foreigner. Even my looks betrayed me. I was small and dark, a Mediterranean man. My speech was different, even in Latin, the common language of scholars. My audience laughed when I pronounced *circulo* in the Italian mode as '*chirculo*'.

Even so, there was a large measure of profit from my visit. My book sold well. My name was talked abroad. I was recognised as a formidable opponent in debate. There was, in all my pleading, a passion that moved even the phlegmatic English.

Castelnau, too, was a passionate man. He loved his wife, adored his children and delighted in his friends, of whom I am still proud to have been one. I admired his tolerance and his curiosity. He was always prepared to stretch his mind to grasp an unfamiliar idea. It was he who suggested a solution to my problems with the Church and with my Order.

"Don't argue theology with them, my friend. You'll lose every time. The Romans have always been jurists at heart. They fit everything—even the ultimate mystery—into the context of law, and then use the law to beat you into submission. So, you are walking down a blind alley. Get out of it, find another road."

"I wish Your Excellency would point it out to me."

"Bend a little. Bow your head if you can't bow your mind. Admit that you were never made for a monk. Beg pardon for your mistakes in an estate to which you know now you were not truly called. Then ask to be released from your vows, ask to be allowed to serve in a simpler role: a scholar-priest under the jurisdiction of a sympathetic bishop. I'm sure we could find you one in France."

"All this, Excellency, is based on supposition."

"Which is?"

"That they want truly to make use of me and not turn me into a cautionary tale."

"You have a point, my friend; but, win or lose, you must play the cards you hold."

"It's a weak hand, Excellency."

"But still enough to keep you in the game. Consider a moment. Here in England you are beyond the reach of Rome. You have the diplomatic protection of France in a Catholic household. You can live in safety, provided you are discreet. On the other hand, you could, if you chose, become a Protestant as your colleague John Florio has done. As a Catholic myself, I cannot recommend it, and my dear wife would most certainly disapprove. You might, at a long stretch, find yourself a chaplaincy in the Church of England—and a wife, too, if you were so disposed, which I sometimes think you are."

"I am always disposed to women, sir. Marriage, I fear, might put as many shackles on me as convent life."

He laughed heartily and added a rejoinder which I was to remember much later.

"Marriage is also an expensive business, my friend—unless the bride has a decent dowry."

"And authors and scholars are not well paid! So, it seems I should need a wealthy bride and a generous patron."

"The bride you must find for yourself."

"And the patron?"

"You are a difficult man to fit, my dear Bruno." He smiled a little ruefully as he said it. "I, myself, find you the most agreeable of companions, but your opinions are not easily understood and, for that matter, not everywhere popular. Patronage is an indulgence of the rich and the powerful. They do not usually like to have hedgehogs in their houses."

It was this remark which prompted me to tell him of Walsingham's suggestion that I become in some fashion a purveyor of political information. Castelnau frowned and shook his head sadly.

"They all do it, Master Bruno. No! I must be honest, *we* all do it in this trade. We live on information. We are like rag pickers, collecting scraps and swatches of discarded cloth, to make patchwork quilts. Who visits whom? And when and why? How does this one suddenly have a full purse, when yesterday he did not have a penny to scratch his backside? Who is in favour with the Queen and who is out? There is not a diplomatic household in the world which does not have its own Judas selling information to people like Walsingham."

"Are you saying you have a Judas in this house, Excellency?"

"Of course. Though I cannot prove him to be so."

"But why keep him then?"

"Because if it is not he, then it will be another. And if you challenge them, they will all give you the same Judas answer: 'Not I, Lord! Never! How could you believe that I would sell you for thirty pieces of silver?' But, believe me, the price is usually much lower than thirty pieces of silver. I know, because I, too, pay for what comes my way."

"So, what would you have me say to Sir Francis Walsingham?"

"What did you say when first he raised the question?"

"I gave him an answer which I hope Your Excellency will approve. I told him I should be happy to oblige him, saving always my obligations and duty and friendship to my host—yourself, Excellency."

"And nothing more was said?"

"Nothing, then or later."

"You know that will not be the end of it."

"Probably not. So, how should I answer if such questions are asked, let us say about activities in this household?"

"Whatever you say, my friend, they will not believe it until they can test it against other information. You say 'yes', they will hear 'no'. You plead ignorance, they will infer knowledge. You refuse to answer, they will presume a traitorous admission."

"It sounds to me, Excellency, very much like my convent in Naples!"

"Exactly so, Master Bruno."

"But why so?"

"Because the same issues are at stake: power, preferences, a greed of wealth or territory, dynastic marriages and all the plots they breed, and whose God is the true God because there is no power but from God and those that be are ordained by God, and therefore by whomever possesses him! You know this, Bruno. Why should I read you sermons?"

"Because you are a man of good heart, Excellency, and I am fortunate in your friendship. I am cursed with a hot temper and a loose tongue, but I shall never betray your trust."

I meant it, every word, but I could not shake off the infection of mistrust which followed on our talk. If there were eavesdroppers in this house, then where could one be safe? It was this unease which made me cling the more closely to the circle of friends into which Castelnau had introduced me.

First and most sympathetic of these was Giovanni Florio, who, in spite of his Italian name and origin, was born in England, and was employed by Castelnau as private secretary and tutor to his daughter. At the time I met him, he had already published a translation of Ramusio's *Voyages of Jacques Cartier* and an Italian-English grammar called *Florio his Firste Fruites,* whose sprightly dialogues were intended as a practice in the language.

He, like me, was a talkative and opinionated fellow. He called himself "the resolute John Florio". Like me, he did not lack detractors, but he was generous to me—most generous in the sharing of his friendships.

Both he and Castelnau enriched my life with friends who thrust me forward, with praise sometimes, but always with new challenges to excellence. Chief among these friends, whom still I remember as the paragon of the perfect gentleman, was Sir Philip Sidney. In his short life—he was killed in a naval battle when he was only thirty-two—he lived many lives, and embellished them all. He was courtier, poet, statesman, soldier, friend and patron of the arts. He had travelled much in Europe and spoke both French and Italian very well. More than all this, however, he had a grace and charm which calmed even my turbulent spirit. He merited respect, but he also offered it and this I value still.

However, it was the poet in him who most attracted me. In this place, where I have seen neither moon nor stars for many years, I still remember lines of his verses:

With how sad steps o moon thou climbest the skies,
How silently and with so wan a face!

And that other single line which summed up so tersely what was happening to me, without my knowing:

"Fool!" said my muse to me "Look on thy heart and write!"

This other self, like Sidney's muse, was urging me to look into my own heart, examine my own mind, accept as authentic my own experience of God in His universe as I perceived it. I still could not reconcile this new self with the old one. I could not yet define the vision I saw or thought I saw. So I continued laboriously to frame it in words.

In London, with the assistance of Sidney and of Castelnau himself, I had found a printer who would issue my works, a man called Charlewood. However, instead of following the usual practice of using his imprint on the binding and on the fly leaves, I yielded to the advice of my friends—and indeed of Charlewood himself—and represented the works, seven in all, as having been printed in Venice or Paris.

Two reasons were offered for this practice: a foreign imprint would sell better than English ones, and the English publisher would avoid the unwelcome attentions of the censors. This little stratagem, harmless enough in all conscience, assumed a large importance at my trial in Venice. It was urged, first, that I was a proven liar whose evidence in defence had no value and, second, that I was a venal man who would do anything for money.

In relative terms, the stratagem was a small default. In fact, it has become another billet of wood to fuel the fire on the day when they burn me! So much for relatives and absolutes in the law and in theology.

My sojourn in England was the happiest and most fruitful period of my life. There are others, many others, who enriched my life, but the list is too long to set down here. I am after all writing a personal apologia and not the history of an age, turbulent and bloody, yet ready to burst into splendour as spring flowers bloom out of a battlefield. The catalogue of my works unrolled itself steadily and with more and more vigour as I wrote in my own tongue: *The Ash Wednesday Supper, Of Cause, Principle and Unity, Of Infinite Universe and Worlds, The Expulsion of the Triumphant Beast.*

I have neither time nor inclination to rehearse them here, but they are in print with the rest of my works. Not all of them will be burned when they burn me. Other generations will read and judge them long after I have been obliterated from the planet. There are moments when I think of this as a revenge: the Inquisitors being forced for ever to chase down my ideas like folly fires in swampland. There is a proverb which says: "Revenge makes a tasty mouthful for the gods." I say rather that truth is its own vindicator and that no one can bury it so deep that it will not rise again, confirmed in glory.

30 December

As I begin to write this day, I am reminded that it is now fourteen years since the abrupt ending of my sojourn in England in the year 1585. This was the manner of it.

On a grey morning in early winter, I was writing in my bedroom at the Embassy. There was nothing to draw me outside. The clouds hung low, a fine rain was falling, there was a stink from the tidal mudflats along the River Thames. So I sat happily at my desk sketching the outline of a new work on the Physics of Aristotle. John Florio came in. He had devastating news—the Ambassador had been recalled to France. His successor would arrive within a month. Our household would be broken up. All of us must make new arrangements for our separate futures.

I asked—somewhat irritably, I confess—why the Ambassador himself had not informed me. Florio, with more patience than he usually displayed, gave me the explanation.

"The despatches from Paris arrived only an hour ago. His Excellency has gone to give the news to his wife. She is ailing, as you know, and she is pregnant again. This change will impose great hardship on her. But there are other concerns, too. His Excellency is in deep financial trouble. Funds which are due to him have not arrived from Paris; nor will they be paid, I think, until he returns there and speaks with the King. More than this, His Excellency has lent large sums of money over the years to Mary, Queen of Scots. There is now little hope that these can or will be repaid. So, be patient, my friend. His Excellency will explain himself in his own time."

"Once he goes, there is nothing for me here. I am naked to the winds. It is time to go. I hope I may travel with him to France."

"Why not propose the idea? I cannot go with him. This is my country. I was born here. I must find another post in England. You, perhaps, could help him on the voyage, but you would have to pay your own passage and settle yourself in Paris."

"I can do that."

I said it confidently enough, but my funds were very low, and my expectations were not high either. Once again, I should have to become a wandering scholar, shouting my wares like a fairground pedlar, bowing and scraping and fawning for patronage. Out of nowhere, a text of scripture came into my head. *And the Lord set a mark on Cain. And Cain went out from the presence of the Lord and dwelt in the land of Nod, on the East of Eden.*

There was a mark on me also. If His Holiness the Pope were God's Vicar, then truly I had left His presence. In that bleak winter moment in London, I did, most desperately, desire to return to it. When I had fled my homeland, I had torn up my roots. They did not take kindly to alien earth, no matter how rich the nourishment it promised. So always, without my being able to define it, I was afflicted with a sense of impermanence, of loss, of alienation. In the days that followed, when I had opportunities for quiet talk with Castelnau, he repeated his counsel, to bow my head in submission and make a truce with Rome. The road to Rome would lead me homeward.

Kindly soul that he was, Castelnau arranged letters of recommendation: one from himself; the other from the Spanish Ambassador to the Apostolic Nuncio in Paris, His Excellency Girolamo Ragazzoni, who was also Bishop of Bergamo. The letters not only explained my personal circumstances, but made warm recommendations as to my character and my future use to the Church, if my current problems could be resolved. It was light armour for a man so heavily besieged, but it was the best Castelnau could offer in his straitened circumstances. He had trials of his own. On the voyage from London, through the complicity of a servant, he was robbed of all his valuables, even of royal gifts. He arrived home penniless and had to set about restoring his fortunes.

In Paris, therefore, our paths diverged more widely. Castelnau kissed hands again at court and was appointed to an army command. I found cheap lodgings in familiar surroundings near the College of Cambrai and renewed old friendships. Françoise Solanges was dead, but my printer friends were still flourishing in spite of the troubles there.

However, I lived lean in the months that followed. I published three small volumes on the Physics of Aristotle, and a work on the Mathematics of Fabrizio Mordente, a compatriot from Salerno who had invented the eight-point compass and written a most exact work called *Compass and Ruler.* His brother, Gaspari, had in fact served with my own father in the militia. Later, Fabrizio and I met again in Prague where he was Imperial Astronomer.

I have asked myself many times over the years why these my friends were able to achieve eminence—or, if they were of noble birth, even idle into it like Sidney in England—while I, with much more to offer than they, found myself continually frustrated in my ambitions and dogged by an obstinate and malignant fate. It took me a long time to understand that the problem was myself and not in any combination of stars. I was like a blinkered horse, seeing only straight ahead, always uneasy in harness and sometimes enraged by checks to my forward course.

My pupil, John Hennequin, had set down a hundred and twenty propositions against the views of Aristotle and his followers on nature and the world. I published these propositions and organised a debate at the College of Cambrai. Hennequin defended the propositions but was bested in debate by a young and brilliant advocate, Raoul Callier.

I was invited to take on Callier—but I declined because the hour was already late. For this, I was derided by the assembly. They demanded I appear again the next day. Again, I declined. I told them I was prepared to concede the victory. Their mockeries were louder and more tumultuous. I knew then, for certain, that the climate of academe and public opinion had changed. The wind and the tide were both against me.

An even worse fate befell me when, one winter's evening, I presented my letters of recommendation and outlined my petition to the Apostolic Nuncio, Ragazzoni, in the presence of his assistant, the Jesuit Spagnolo. My petition was simple: that the censures against me be lifted, that I be admitted again to the sacraments and to the practice of the priestly office—not in my Order, but in the secular ministry. His Excellency was urbane. He heard me without comment, but he held out little hope. He told me his intervention would be untimely and unsuccessful. When I begged to know why, he said:

"Brother Giordano, there are certain realities you must accept. Since April, a new Pontiff sits on the throne of Peter: His Holiness Pope Sixtus the Fifth. Like you, he is a member of an ancient Order, the Franciscans. Unfortunately for you, he has served as an Inquisitor—Grand Inquisitor of Venice, no less! He is not—let me say it with great respect—a man of mild disposition. Already he has begun a ruthless regime of purgation in Italy. He has imposed the death penalty for banditry, incest, procuration, abortion, sodomy and even adultery. He does not spare even those close to him. So, Brother Giordano, we are not talking here of a gentle pastor shepherding his flock or seeking out lost lambs to carry them home on his shoulders. This is a man with a flail in his hands, winnowing the grain on the threshing floor! I tell you plainly, there is no hope for you except in full submission. Return to your Order, beg pardon, accept whatever penance is laid upon you, let your superiors intercede for you with the Holy Father. Are you prepared for that?"

I told him I was not. I had nothing but unhappy memories of life in the Order. His Excellency shrugged and spread his soft hands in regret and deprecation of my folly.

"Then I regret, I can do nothing for you, Brother Giordano."

The interview was over. I was dismissed into the outer darkness of the damned. I spent the rest of that night in a brothel.

It was not my first visit to a house of appointment—nor, thank God, my last. I held the view that if my ministry was in suspense, so was my always precarious commitment to chastity. The house was one I had frequented, sometimes alone, sometimes with friends, in my more prosperous days as Reader at the King's court. Now, it was a very expensive indulgence.

I remember the woman well. She was called *la petite guenon*, the little monkey, because she was practised and playful and full of cheerful mischief. I was desperate to bury my grief in her body, and after the first wild moments, I clung to her, waking and sleeping, through a very long night.

Seven years of prison life and prison diet have sapped my strength and dimmed my desire. Dante was right when he wrote: *There is no greater grief than to remember happy times in misery.* Yet, I still remember that night, not for the pleasure of it—how long does the memory of sexual ecstasy endure?—but for the strange and quite magical moment of revelation which I experienced in the small hours of the morning.

The circumstances were trivial and even sordid. I eased myself away from the woman sleeping beside me and got up to piss in the chamber pot. Before I climbed back into bed, I stood naked at the window, looking out at a clear winter sky, full of bright stars. Suddenly, I understood what I needed to say, what I had been trying to say all those years in Latin, in Italian, in writing and by word of mouth, but which I had never managed to articulate fully.

It was an Archimedian moment in which my spirit cried out: "Eureka. I have found it." It was a biblical moment, too, when I heard a voice that said "open your mouth" and my halting tongue was suddenly eloquent.

I was no longer—humankind was no longer—locked in the closed circles of Ptolemy's or Copernicus's universe. We were not at the centre of it, either. We were not a single system, we were the smallest part of a vast creation, expanding to infinity. Our world was only one of uncounted worlds each in motion in its own orbit. It was the vastness of this vision which finally made the notion of God intelligible, which, indeed, made us intelligible to ourselves, and the terrors of our lives tolerable.

I do not know how long I stood there, but suddenly I was trembling, with cold, yes, but also with the shock of the experience. I climbed back into bed. The woman stirred and turned to me and we folded ourselves again each into the other.

This, it seemed to me, was the final coda of the revelation. We were not separate. Nothing in the cosmos was separate or disconnected. None of it could fall out of the hands of the Creator who had made it, who infused it, and was immanent in all its parts. For the first time in years, I said a real prayer. "Give me memory to hold this moment. Give me words to tell it."

When, early in the morning, I walked back to my lodgings, I was still in a trance. I knew what I wanted to accomplish; but I knew also that I needed a time of calm, a freedom from financial worries, a certain distance from the tumults which were rising again in France. Immediate question: where to find all these things at once?

Clearly, I had to look eastward and northward, to those centres of learning in Germany where the Reformers had taken strong hold, and scholars like Philipp Melanchthon were reviving the study of original sources in Hebrew and Greek.

I went first to Marburg-on-the-Lahn because there in 1527 Philip the Magnificent had founded the first Protestant university and there, two years later, the same landgrave Philip invited Luther and Zwingli and Melanchthon to lead a colloquy on the essential articles of faith which might constitute a common confession for the Reformers of Germany and Switzerland.

The climate, therefore, seemed auspicious—an enlightened prince, a new university, an open-minded scholarship, even in contentious subjects. So, to Marburg I went, armed with my published works, a carefully edited curriculum of my career, and a pocketful of hopes.

My welcome seemed warm enough. On 25 July 1586, I was matriculated. I paid my fee and was signed into the register of the university as "Jordanus Nolan, a Neapolitan, Doctor of Roman Theology, admitted with the agreement of the faculty".

I have always suspected that it was the phrase 'Roman Theology' which did the damage. When, as the next step, I applied formally for permission to teach philosophy in public, the Rector refused it point blank. He also refused to give his reasons, saying that whatever they were, the faculty agreed with them.

I was affronted and enraged by this patent untruth. I went to the Rector's house and upbraided him for an act contrary to all justice and to common practice in all universities. He refused to discuss the matter further. He refunded my fee, and I was once more on the road, northward this time to Wittenberg where Martin Luther had nailed his ninety-five theses to the door of the Schlosskirche, and where later he and his friend and advocate, Melanchthon, were buried side by side.

There was another good omen also. My old friend and compatriot, the jurist Alberico Gentilis, was here. He arranged that I should deliver a private lecture to some persons of importance. As a result, I was engaged to lecture at the university for a period of two years.

So far, so good, but every rose has its thorns, and that which irked me most was my own incompetence in the German language, and my small acquaintance with local habits and customs. To be sure we all had Latin, the common language of scholastics, but for bed and board and recreation, the common tongue serves best. I was, therefore, always two steps behind both the history and the current growth of the Reform movement which Martin Luther had launched in Germany. I could not measure the strength of his vernacular writing and preaching. Some things, however, I did understand clearly: that he had confronted Pope and Emperor and rebels within his own faction and survived them all while under excommunication, outlawry, and even the threat of assassination.

I made myself familiar with the twenty-eight articles of the Augsburg Confession, of which Philipp Melanchthon was the principal author and which was intended to demonstrate that Luther's doctrines were in no wise a departure from the fundamental tenets of Christian faith. I admired the clarity and the tolerance of the exposition. I, myself, would have found no difficulty in subscribing to it—although I felt that we had to reach much further and stretch more widely to embrace the boundless wonder of the testimony written in the earth itself and in the night sky.

Nonetheless, I confess that I taught in Wittenberg with more discretion and less controversy because of the freedom and the respect which were granted to me. My friend Gentilis had wisely suggested that my lectures should take account of the new currents in German thought and the distance theology had travelled from the deductive dogmas of Aristotle. My audiences, private and public, included the sons of noble houses, academics, professors and doctors. They welcomed me with open arms and honoured me as a friend and colleague.

The works I wrote in this time of contentment were largely academic in character because I had a guaranteed circle of readers, and because my lectures were prepared with extra care and subtlety. Still, I meditated every day on the project which had presented itself to me that winter's night in the bedroom of *la petite guenon* in Paris. This was something I could not force; it had to grow like a strong tree, in its own time.

In Wittenberg, I found lodging in the house of one Wolf Springer, a retired professor of mathematics who continued to tutor a small group of advanced students. He was a portly, puffing fellow, who ate too much and drank too heartily, but whose brain was still sharp. He worked out of a small studio at the university, so that we met only for supper and a game of chess, at which he was a master and I a very poor pupil. My head was always in the clouds of speculation while his was intent on the mathematics of the game. When he had me in check, he would take his candle and go to bed, leaving me to find a way out of the trap into which he had led me.

Springer was a widower, but his house was kept by an unmarried daughter, Greta, an attractive but laconic young woman who kept a spotless house and a generous table and bullied her father and me into a not altogether disagreeable servitude. She was also an accomplished seamstress and a skilled glove-maker. While we played our nightly game, she would sit in the pool of lamplight, stitching placidly, listening to our talk and making an occasional pointed interjection of her own. Schooled by her father, she wrote a good clerkly hand in the Gothic mode, read fluently in German and Latin and kept her accounts as accurately as any banker.

She quizzed me about my career. I was happy to describe it—most of it, at least—in colourful detail. She did not seem overly impressed. What interested her most was my life at court in Paris and London: what the women wore, how they conducted their social lives, how they managed their marriages and love affairs. Philosophy bored her, she told me. Religion was a matter of good manners and social custom. It was like her father's mathematics, the expression of an orderly creation. She could not understand why there was so much trouble and strife about formulae and credal expressions. She made it very clear that she would have no religious contention in her house. I told her she should not fear it from me.

These terse and somewhat disjointed conversations were spread over several nights after her father had retired to bed. Finally, she made the questions more personal.

"Are there no women in your life, Master Bruno?"

"There have been. At this moment, there is none."

"Are you not lonely?"

"We are all lonely, sometimes. For wanderers like myself, it is difficult to sustain an attachment."

"Are you saying that it is easy for stay-at-homes like me?"

There was an edge of anger in her voice which surprised me. I needed a quarrel as little as I needed the Black Death. I tried to mollify her.

"Please! I meant no more than I said. I am a newcomer in your house. You asked me a simple question. I tried to answer it. Let's talk about you."

"There is nothing to say. I am what you see, a dutiful daughter, mistress in the house my mother left me."

"Where Giordano Bruno, the man from a far county, is happy to be sheltered and cared for."

She smiled at that. The awkward moment was passed. I bade her goodnight and went to my room. I left her alone in the lamp-light, measuring a piece of fine leather against the paper pattern for a glove.

The tricks that memory plays on us are sometimes very strange. As I made ready for bed that night, I found myself musing on my boyhood days in Nola, on the forests and vineyards of Mount Cicada and the dark, distant shape of Vesuvius which marked the end of my world. At the heart of my musing was a single thought: Mount Cicada was my place. I belonged to it. My household gods were there. That was why, wherever I lodged, I inscribed myself "Giordano Bruno the Nolan". That was why I found a curious pathos in Greta Springer's remark: "I am what you see, a dutiful daughter, mistress in the house my mother left me."

I, on the other hand, had no inheritance, no family either, because on the day I took my vows I had renounced them both. I had made myself a poor man for Christ. I had been adopted into the brotherhood of the chosen who would preach his message to the world.

Now, on every term of the bargain, I was out of pocket. I could not, I dared not, return to the past. My present was an imperma-nence, my fortune a large interrogation mark. I put on my nightshirt, pinched out the candle and huddled for warmth under the bed covers. I lay there a long time, restless in the dark, staring at the starlight through the attic window.

My small passage-at-arms with Greta Springer had defined more strictly my personal dilemma. She was the unmarried daughter, destined by fate and custom to care for an ageing parent. She was adequately endowed with the ownership of the house; but clearly the dowry was counterbalanced by the condition that she remain in residence and continue to care for a father still vigorous in health and active in his profession.

It was natural, therefore, that she should see me as a potential marriage partner. I was the scholar-in-residence, just across the passage from her bedroom. The father approved me, and he, too, had a use for me as a resident son-in-law to keep his household stable. The situation offered me, also, a series of benefits. If I chose to join the Lutheran communion, I could shrug off the censures of Rome, contract a valid marriage, and, under the patronage of the Elector Augustus, secure a permanent residence in the country.

I knew that one word from me would settle the whole issue: betrothal, marriage, conversion, a new and settled life. Yet, the word stuck in my gullet. In my present perilous state, I ask myself why the devil I did not utter it!

At the time, I had a whole list of ready answers. I was still young. My fortunes were at last on the upswing. Times were changing. Rome itself would change. I was the Nolan, a man from the south. I could not see myself living for ever under the grey clouds of the Northland, walking soberly to church each Sunday with my wife on my arm, doffing my scholar's cap to a dour Lutheran congregation. I could not imagine shaping my words to a new rhythm. I would not cut my thoughts to a new measure for a new audience, just as critical, just as contentious as the old. I had little reason to love the Romans, but I understood very well what Erasmus meant when he announced: *I will stay in this Church until I find a better.* To which I added a gloss of my own: "This is the skin into which I was born. I cannot, I will not, change colour like a chameleon to match the hue of the leaves."

Beyond all this, I had to admit that I had as little talent for marriage as I had for conventual life. A philosopher is by nature a vagabond spirit. Grammarians and jurists and theologians are bound by data and definitions and dogmas.

In spite of all the charges they have brought against me, I am not a heresiarch, greedy for power over his followers. I am not a Doctor Faustus who pledged his soul to the devil for enlightenment. I am, at worst, a puzzled pilgrim, looking for a cap to keep the sun from boiling his brains. The problem was—and still is—that every hatter wants to slap his own brand of bonnet on my head, whether it fits or not. Then, for final insult, each one expects me to wear his own cockade as well!

All my training in the Order of Friars Preachers, and in the intellectual life which it fostered, seemed directed to the surrender of my primal self and to its ultimate extinguishment in an act of suicidal immolation. What they wanted to produce were loyal servants of an institution which was bonded directly to Rome, beyond the jurisdiction of provincial bishops, whose loyalties, being local, were always suspect. The Order itself profited from the bonding. It was protected, enriched and given immense delegations of power, not least that of the Inquisition itself. In this process of high governance, there was no place for erratic individuals like myself. Yet, they would not let me out; they would keep me in, to destroy me in the end.

All this is a far cry from my bedtime conversation with Greta Springer in Wittenberg those many years ago. Yet, it is all part of the same story. I would not put new shackles on myself; yet I would not lay shame on her either. I should like to think that will make one small credit for me on judgement day.

In this solitude where I now dwell, where I have dwelt for seven weary years, I have come to at least one firm conviction. The first gift we are given, and the last we surrender, is the self, that essence which distinguishes each of us from all others, that life which is solely ours. In my cell, there is only that self and the Creator who gave it being. I did not ask for the gift. I got it, willy nilly, and I am still paying off the debt, month by painful month. At the end, I shall have to hand back the gift, diminished, defaced, yet still, I hope, bearing the legible imprint of the Maker. Fragments of the verses I wrote years ago sound in my head once more.

> *There was in me,*
> *That which no future century*
> *Will deny: That I did not fear to die,*
> *That I preferred a courageous death to a*
> *non-combatant life.*

Eh! Eh! Eh! Brave words, Brother Giordano, while the candle flame still burns, and you huddle in the small pool of light. But when you snuff out the light and the darkness leaps in from every corner, and the poor crazed creature three cells away begins his screaming, what then?

Would not the spinster daughter and the mathematical father, and the stolid burghers of Wittenberg have been a better choice? It is too late now. The moving finger has written on the wall: *Mene Mene Tekel Upharsin.* The days of my life are numbered and nearly over. The Inquisitors have weighed me in their scales and found me wanting. The little kingdom I have built, that small pile of books and pamphlets and poems, will be burned in front of Saint Peter's and my own ashes will be shovelled up and tossed into the Tiber. As well now that I have no woman of my own, else she would be reduced to beggary for the crime of having loved me. As well that I have sired no children—at least none that I know of—so no one will have to grieve for me.

When they burn you like this, they do not even leave you a coin to pay the ferryman. You are blotted out of the book of the living. That little self, that wandering child who roamed the green slopes of Mount Cicada, will be consigned into the care of the God who made him. At very worst, He has to be less frightening than those who order things in His name.

I have blasphemed often, but never against him who said: *Let the children come to me; the kingdom of heaven belongs to them.*

31 December

It is New Year's Eve. Tomorrow it will be *capodanno* and the beginning of a new century, the seventeenth of what we are pleased to call the Christian Era. Outside, my gaoler tells me, it is bitterly cold, with a freezing wind howling down from the Apennines. The shepherds, who come down each winter from the Abruzzi to pasture their flocks in the Campagna, huddle with their sheep and their dogs in the angles of ancient walls and the hollows of ruined vaults. Usually, they take to the streets in this season, playing their bagpipes to earn wine money. Today, their fingers and their pipes are frozen.

Inside the prison, it is always cold, but at least we are out of the wind. We hear its howling as a ghostly whisper, like the plaint of a lost soul. When I have emptied my bucket and eaten my meagre collation, I am tempted to go back to bed, pull the blanket over my head and hibernate like a bear. Indeed, I have sometimes compared myself to one of those dancing bears I saw at country fairs in Germany. The poor animal has a ring in its snout, and in the ring there is a goad, so that every time his master tugs upon the rope, the animal dances, not with joy but with pain.

This is how my life has been passed for years now. Each session with the Inquisitors—a repetitive torment in itself—is preceded by a sharp reminder that the *strappado* is still an active instrument of interrogation. It is the bleak consolation of my situation, that my next encounter will not be with the torturer but with the executioner. So I tell myself that I am not a carnival beast but a man. I wrap my blanket about my shoulders, seat myself at my table and take up again the disjointed narrative of my life and labours.

For centuries now, it has been a fact of life that scholars and artists and poets must live by the patronage of the rich and powerful. In our day, the richest and most powerful patron is the Church. After the Church, in their various orders and degrees, come kings and princes and nobles and latterly those prosperous merchants and lucky adventurers who have been ennobled by wealth itself.

There is a consequence that follows from this: if you want to share the patron's meal you have to find a place at the table, above the salt, rather than below it. In Wittenberg, for nearly two years, I was a table guest. I earned money and respect and, most important of all, I had leisure and a free mind for study and writing.

I had, however, forgotten that when a patron dies, his successor changes the list of clients and the table placement changes as well. That is exactly what happened to me in Wittenberg.

The Elector Augustus of Saxony was an elderly man, a Lutheran by profession and sympathy. When he died in 1586, the power in the Protestant camp passed to the Calvinist zealot, John Casimir, who effectively dominated the new Elector Christian 1. Very soon, Casimir and Christian began to weed out alien or suspect elements in the Church and at the university. Naturally enough, my name was high on the list. I was an ultramontane, born and nurtured on the wrong side of the Alps. It was intimated to me that I had a choice between an honourable exit or a troubled one. I chose the former, and asked permission to mark the occasion by a valedictory oration of praise and thanks to the Rector, the faculty and the distinguished fellows at the university who had welcomed me, the stranger, into their midst.

It was an arrangement that suited everyone. My thanks were genuine. My friends were pleased. No one was shamed. My personal reputation was enhanced. I swallowed my sadness and my anger, but I celebrated them in a small epigram from Ecclesiastes, which I dedicated and signed for certain friends:

What is? What was.
What was? What is:
There is nothing new under the sun.

Once again, I took to the road. This time, I headed east to the Imperial city of Prague in Bohemia, where my friend, Fabrizio Mordente, was Imperial Astronomer and Mathematician to the Emperor Rudolf II. I knew he would receive me well, and introduce me to a circle of gentlemen who would be prepared, as they had been in the other places, to pay me for private lectures, and buy copies of my works. Even so, it was late in the day for me. This was 1588. I was forty years old, yet I was still like Cain, a wanderer in the lands east of Eden.

Strangely enough, I was not irked by the travel itself. I revelled in the newness of places, the variety of mankind and womankind along the highroads of Europe, the gossip of coachmen and ostlers and the warm, beery smell of taverns and post houses. I developed a kind of *lingua franca* which enabled me to talk with them. The old skills of commerce with strangers, which I had learned in the lanes and alleys of Naples, came back to me. On the road I was never bored. And it was not hard to find a woman, serving maid or travelling matron to warm my bed and thank me in the morning for my company. I was grateful for the respite from loneliness and I was learning at every moment, fitting the fragments of new knowledge into the framework of a bold philosophy, beyond the categories and the syllogisms of the schoolmen.

This was the work which I was still writing in my head while I prepared my more prosaic offerings: a tract on Lullian Medicine, a commentary on the Physics of Aristotle, the Principles and Elements of Geometry. These were pamphlets rewritten or reconstructed from earlier works, but they were at once my passports to academe, and my petitions for imperial patronage.

In Prague, a handsome city, Fabrizio Mordente welcomed me warmly and lodged me in his house until I found my own place. He was, like myself, a southerner. The dialect of Salerno is not too different from Neapolitan and it was a very special pleasure to talk freely in the language of our home place. Mordente's wife played most sweetly on the lute, and after supper in the evenings, we sang the old songs of the seashore and the countryside: "*Sto core mio, Villanella ch'all' acqua va, Michelemma…*" These little domestic events filled me with a joy at first, but they left me with a haunting sense of loss, the melancholy which the exile never wholly loses.

Fabrizio Mordente understood the emotion very well, and he understood, too, the special risks of my position. He explained them in good-humoured fashion.

"My friend, nobody quarrels with mathematicians or geometers. For one thing, they can't read our equations and for another, they can't measure a piece of land or build a church steeple without us. They don't object when we borrow our algebra from the Arabs and our symbols from the Greeks and our stellar observations from the Persians. Nobody quarrels with a physician, either. If the patient lives, he is a wonder-worker and he pockets the pay and wears the credit. If the patient dies, it is God who has called him, not the doctor who has killed him. But your case, my dear Giordano, is quite, quite different. First, you are dealing with invisibles, intangibles. You cannot measure an idea. You cannot weigh it like flour in a bag. When you put words to it, the words mean different things to different people. There is as much difference in their meaning as there is between a stone hatchet and a fine steel axe. Most perilous of all, my friend, you are an eloquent man. You move people, you stir them like fire in the blood."

"Is that a bad thing, Fabrizio? Is that a crime?"

"No. But it is a dangerous talent. Think a little—a single speech can bring down an empire, a single hymn can split a Church. What do the people prefer to hear—plain chant from the cloister or Martin Luther's hymn: *A mighty fortress is our God?*"

"But I do not preach either revolt or reform. I ask only for liberty to think and to explain."

"To those who rule, ideas are dangerous and can threaten to topple the throne."

"Are you saying I shall not be welcome here in Prague?"

"In this house, you are always welcome. For the rest, I have already spoken of you to my friend, Gian Maria della Lama, who is personal physician to the Emperor. He is also a Neapolitan, so you will be comfortable with him. He will receive you courteously as my friend and present you to the Emperor as a distinguished scholar. You will offer the dedication of the new works you have brought, as a tribute to His Imperial Majesty. According to della Lama, His Majesty will accept the dedication, since the books are technical treatises and contain no contentious matter."

"And then?"

"His Majesty will offer you a gift to acknowledge your compliment."

"What sort of gift may I expect?"

"I am assured it will be generous."

"A post at the university, a resident fellowship?"

"Regrettably, no. The university is a Catholic institution, His Majesty is a Catholic prince. You will be given money and compliments, of course—and recommended to enjoy your brief stay in this wonderful city."

"How brief, Fabrizio?"

"No more than six months. Preferably less."

"Dear God! What do I do next? Where do I go?"

"You have time to think about that. Talk to della Lama, he has had problems of his own with Rome, but he has survived them very well. One thing I know he will tell you. What profits more here is *bella figura:* a certain style, eh?"

Mordente was right, of course. It was up to me to build a triumph out of my disappointment. I must not be seen as a down-at-heel academic, begging for a new appointment. On the contrary, I was a distinguished scholar, enjoying a period of quiet study while I put the finishing touches on a masterwork. I was beginning to learn, albeit too late in life, that ambition might be attained by seeming to abjure it, and that reputation might be most securely founded on careful anonymity.

Gian Maria della Lama commended my discretion and revealed to me the nature of his own experience. His appointment as Imperial Physician had roused great jealousies, not only in his profession but in the Roman Curia. After all, the man who tended the Imperial body came closer to him than any other of his counsellors in Church or State. The jealousies begot malicious rumours, which were reported to the Inquisition and to the Pontiff himself.

"My own fault in part," della Lama admitted frankly. "I opened my mouth too wide in the wrong company. I said that the Church canonises its own saints, invents its own heretics and authenticates its own miracles. The only thing it can't do is invent its own medical science, much as it would like to do so. You can imagine, Master Bruno, what they made of that! Immediately I was delated on suspicion of heresy. His Holiness, Pope Sixtus, who is, as you know, a furious watchdog of the faith, wrote a letter to the Emperor, telling him that only good Catholics should be admitted to the intimacy of the Imperial sick bed. Fortunately for me, the Emperor refused to bend, but he did warn me that neither the Pontiff nor the Inquisitors would easily forget or forgive. He granted me permanent residence in Bohemia and suggested I stay far away from Italy. I have bought a small estate just outside the city and I am now a citizen of this country."

This avowal encouraged me to open my own heart to him, and he gave me careful counsel.

"Once the Emperor has received you and shown you his favour, do not frequent the court, do not make yourself in any fashion a public figure. That will please the Emperor. He will make it known that the presence of so great a scholar does honour to the city and that your desire for studious solitude should be respected."

"Can you suggest where I might find this studious solitude?"

"You would be welcome to stay at my villa. There is a married couple who take care of it for me. She controls the staff, he manages the farm. They would make you very comfortable. There is a good library and a stable of passable horses, if you choose to ride. There is plenty of room, and when my family and I come—which is all too rarely these days—we shall enjoy the pleasure of your company. Well, what do you say?"

What could I say but my thanks, which were redoubled when the Emperor accepted the dedication of my works and made me a most generous gift—a purse of three hundred thalers, more than enough to maintain me for a year. He also suggested, in case I should be interested, that his princely neighbour, Duke Julius of Brunswick, had just founded a new academy in Helmstedt and given it his own name: the Julian Academy. Clearly, they wanted to build up a strong faculty. His Majesty would be happy to commend me to Duke Julius. If I chose to write to the academy, he would send my letter by Imperial courier—no small favour when courier post was ruinously expensive and not always punctual or reliable.

It was an answer, however temporary, to all my problems: a tranquil retreat, free board and lodging, a chance to address myself to the masterwork whose sonorous rhythms were already echoing in my skull.

Spring had already arrived when I took up residence in the country and, under the watchful eye of the châtelaine, laid out my books and manuscripts at a window that looked out on orchards in bloom and the greening of hills beyond. For a brief magical hour, I could believe I was back in my childhood on Mount Cicada.

When inspiration flagged, I addressed myself to a small compendium of works on magic, natural, mathematical and malevolent. These, I thought, would make a suitable accompaniment to the letter I proposed to write to the Rector of the new Julian Academy in Helmstedt. What I did not know at the time was that these works would figure in later charges against me. A man who dealt in magic was properly called a magus, a magician. A magus was, in the popular mind, or in the mind of any whom it would profit to claim so, a dealer in black arts and forbidden mysteries. This was what my traitorous patron, Mocenigo, later wanted to buy from me: the key to mystery. When I would not sell it, because I could not, he sold me instead to the Inquisition.

In that moment, however, in my country retreat, I was happy. My head was clear. My body was well nourished with country food. I was free at last from that nagging, desperate concern about tomorrow. I was writing freely. The first drafts of *De monade* and *De immenso* were piling up on my desk. I made few erasures. The prose and the verse poured out in a flood, carrying my thoughts with them, lively as fish in clear water.

> *The divine essence is all in all. It fills everything, pervades every-thing.*
>
> *This is the life of lives, the soul of souls. There are two active principles of motion. The one finite and moving in time. The other infinite, which is the nature of the Soul of the World, of Divinity in fact, which is everywhere and in everything.*

I did not need any longer the tricks and artifices of literary composition, the elaborate metaphors, the fashionable mythologies. What I sought now was clarity and accuracy in the expression of vast simplicities and the infinities hidden in a dust mote or a grain of sand.

I longed for a moment when I could abdicate the past and the present and commit myself, free as an eagle, to the high winds of speculative thought. I thought that if I had a place like this, a small farm to feed me and some service to sustain me, I could become the philosopher of a new age. If I could free myself from the tyranny of patronage and subsist on the revenue of my books and the produce of my small-holding, I could, I believed, astonish the world.

It was this surge of euphoria which brought me to a fateful decision. I would make one more excursion into academe. I would take the Emperor's advice, write to Helmstedt and ask the Rector to matriculate me and permit me to teach until I had completed my masterwork. After that, I should go to Frankfurt, publish the work and then take a new tack, which Mordente had suggested to me: find a banker to finance me into a viable smallholding, and then make a deal with a publishing house like Wechel and Fischer in Frankfurt, to give continuity to my works and to my income.

The more I thought of it, the more possible it seemed, but I needed two steps: into Helmstedt and out again. An Imperial recommendation of my scholarship was too valuable to waste, and a year's academic salary would preserve my small capital for the great venture ahead.

As I dreamed it, as I planned it, so it did come to pass. Early in the autumn of 1588, I made my farewells in Prague and journeyed to Helmstedt where, on 13 January 1589, I was matriculated into the Julian Academy, which at the time of my enrolment had five thousand students and more than fifty masters.

I was told that I would be considered for a teaching post in due course. Meantime, I settled myself in lodgings, gathered around myself a small group of fee-paying disciples and continued with the next part of my works in progress, *De immenso*. This, by a most bitter irony, is the work on which they will most surely convict me of heresy, since it deals with a proposition as yet unthinkable—an infinite universe and a plurality of worlds, created and maintained in being by an immanent Divinity.

However, in Helmstedt, thank God, I had no chart to read the future, although I could not wholly escape the controversies of the present. In May, Duke Julius died. His obsequies were celebrated with much pomp—and most evident sincerity—in the fortress chapel. I took no part in these events, other than as a spectator; but seven weeks later, at the end of the official period of mourning, I offered myself to deliver the customary Oration of Consolation which would close the ceremonies. My offer was accepted. I spent time and care, indeed a great deal of emotion, on the text. I owed much to the kindness of this good man, and to the welcome he had offered me in his city. I spoke without reserve:

> "I came here to pursue noble aspirations and studies, which I valued the more because in my own country I had been

exposed to the greedy maw of the Roman wolf, forced into an unhealthy and superstitious cult, oppressed by the violence of tyranny. Here in Helmstedt, I have been, as if by a miracle, returned to life. I have felt myself to be a free citizen, secure in the enjoyment of a thousand courtesies and honours."

The oration so pleased Duke Henry Julius that he made me a gift of eighty scudi and guaranteed me his personal protection against my adversaries, among whom, ironically enough, was one Gilbert Voet, Chief Pastor and Superintendent of the church in Helmstedt.

This arrogant fellow had taken it upon himself to render a public judgement in a private dispute by excommunicating me from the Lutheran assembly, of which I had never been formally a member. Voet was one of those litigious and self-righteous fellows who are found in every religious sect. However, the intervention of the duke silenced him, although it did not suppress his enmity towards me, nor the zeal with which he continued to plot against me.

These two events, the improvement in my personal fortune, and the inescapable religious friction, confirmed me in my plan to finish all my works in progress, and use them as the foundation of a new and independent career.

To this end, I employed a secretary, a young graduate from the university called Jerome Besler, son of the Protestant Pastor of Sprottau in Silesia. He was studious, discreet and industrious. I was able to dictate to him, instead of engaging always in the crabbed labour of handwriting, and his loyal companionship was important to me in that busy and critical year.

To Besler, I dictated the final versions of my works on magic and another volume on the *Origins and Elements of Things and their Causes*. With him, also, I discussed and made constant critical changes to the three key works: *De monade*, *De immenso* and *De universo et mondi*.

This was the labour in which I was happiest, the nearest a man can come to a divine creative act: conjuring something out of nothing, or, perhaps less presumptuously, imposing a creative order on a confused mass of ideas and imaginings.

I was tired now of arguments and disputations and all the mock tournaments of scholars in which they display their skills like fighting cocks before an audience of the ignorant. I craved then what I have now in too great abundance: a leisure for solitude and contemplation.

The day is almost over, and I am just lighting my candle when the door of my cell is thrust open and the guard admits my friend, Brother John, the almoner, the *homunculus Britannicus* who serves the Master General. His cornflower eyes shine with good humour. I hurry to embrace him and greet him with almost tearful pleasure.

"Brother John! This is a wonderful surprise. I never expected to see you again. What brings you here?"

"My own two feet and the indulgence of the Master General, to whom I made certain humble representations."

"Such as?"

"Tomorrow is a feast day, the beginning of a new year. It's an appropriate time to visit the sick and those in prison. You are still like Jacob, wrestling with the dark angel and being hurt in the struggle. Your brethren should be here to help—one of us, at least!"

"And how did the Master General take that little sermon?"

"Better than I expected. Indeed, he sends you a personal gift, a rosary which he himself has blessed. When you recite the Paters and Aves, he asks that you remember him."

"Which I shall not fail to do. Tell him that."

"I shall. Meantime, I've brought the gifts of the poor—wine and sausage. A bottle to share and a bottle to save."

He hoists up the skirt of his gown and shows me the gifts, hidden, as before, in the fishnet bag around his waist. Among them is a corkscrew, a bundle of goose quills and, wonder of wonders, a small penknife, the first I have had since my imprisonment. Brother John cautions me.

"Hide the knife. When I was here last, I saw that you were

writing. A scribe must be able to cut his own quills—even if others mutilate his ideas!"

As he lays out the gifts on my table and uncorks the bottle we are to share, I ask myself how far I can trust this man and how much I am prepared to gamble on him. I have suffered before when the Inquisitors have lodged me with informers to provoke me to indiscretions. But, somehow, I cannot read this little man as a spy or a *provocatore*. Besides, what in truth am I risking? My life is already forfeit. My memorial, on which I set so much store, what is it? At worst, an indulgence; at best, a fragile hostage to the fortunes of centuries, the ravages of too many tomorrows.

As we drink the first bottle, and chew on slices of country sausage, I ask:

"Brother John, would you be willing to receive my confession?"

"More than willing, Brother Giordano."

"Under the seal?"

"How else?"

"Even if, at the end, you felt you could not offer me absolution?"

"What makes you think I would refuse it?"

"The manner, or even the time, in which I make the confession. Perhaps after I have been cast out of the Church, perhaps because of the defective form in which I might offer it."

He gives me a long quizzical look, then a shining smile and shakes his head.

"The casting out, all the anathemas, are curses which we, the righteous ones, call down upon ourselves. I am your brother, not your judge. I absolve you, as I hope to be absolved, in the name of God—but I am not God to withhold or to offer mercy. As to the manner of the act, you can make a single sign or recite all the penitential psalms, it makes no difference. Do you want to do it now?" He smiles again. "We could hardly be more private."

Then, because I still hesitate, he challenges me gently.

"You find it hard to trust me. Is that it?"

"Call it a prison infection. I find it hard to trust anyone. But, I beg you, do not be insulted."

"And you will not be insulted if I refuse to persuade you to trust?"

"Of course not."

"So, where are we, Brother Giordano? In a blind alley?"

"It seems so."

"Let me try then to walk us out of it, saving always your right to remain silent and commit your cause to God alone."

"I would like that, yes."

"So, let's begin with me, Brother John, the almoner, the little man who transports his gifts slung around his crotch. I was always the runt in my mother's litter, small and misshapen. As a boy, I was mocked and bullied, but I was a reasonable scholar for the Black Friars. When I grew older, the convent seemed a good place to be. It offered safety, fraternal care, the protection and the dignity of the holy habit of Saint Dominic. I was not disappointed. I found all those things and I was, I am, grateful. But, like everyone who has been abused, I remained a sceptic, never quite believing that I could hold on to my good fortune. I am still a sceptic, but I have one talent which you have never acquired, a talent for silence and accommodation. I am not always proud of it, but most of the time, yes, I am, because it is a talent for survival—and the first condition of salvation itself is that we survive to attain it. So, you see, in this we are very alike; except that you are a slow learner in the art of silent endurance."

"How right you are, Brother John. How right you are!"

"Please. Let me continue. There are others like our Master General, like many others in the Church, who have an opposite talent: the talent for belief. They call it 'the gift of faith' as if it were a sweetmeat given to good children for reward. They're fortunate! Give them safe premises, they'll draw a safe conclusion, then pull the shutters down and say 'Our light is plenty for the road to Paradise'. Hand them a torch, they'll set the world on fire and call it Christendom no matter who gets burned."

"If the Inquisition could hear you now, Brother John, you'd be the one to burn!"

"But there is no one here, Brother Giordano, save thee and me and God, who is our silent witness."

"And what does He think of it?"

"He said it centuries ago of the ones who killed him. 'Father, forgive them. They don't know what they are doing.' Pass me the bottle like a good man, and pour another cup for yourself. One to drink and one to save, remember?"

It was then, while I was still sober, that I decided to trust him. I slit the sacking of my pallet, took out the pages of my manuscript and laid them on the table in front of him.

"There's my confession, Brother, under the seal as you promised. It's not finished yet, but it will be before they kill me."

He scans the pages swiftly, pausing now and then to weigh a passage which has caught his special attention. Then, he asks:

"What do you want me to do with it?"

"Take it out of this place. Find a safe home for it, from whence it may emerge one day into the light."

"Why is that so important to you?"

"I do not want to be erased from history, without a word written in my defence."

"A reasonable demand. How will you deliver this to me?"

"You will collect it yourself, because I shall ask for you to receive my final confession. This, I think, they will not refuse me, though you, my brother, are free to refuse both the service and the sacrament."

"I shall be glad to offer both, Brother Bruno. I shall begin to work quietly on the Master General. He will be pleased when I tell him that you are at least in the way of salvation. I believe he will encourage my visits to you. I think that even he is beginning to feel guilty about this long sad affair."

"But he will make no effort to save me?"

"That would be too much to hope. He is the head of a great and powerful Order, but he holds his own power by delegation only.

He will not challenge the Pontiff or the Curia. You must not blame him too much. He is more a prisoner than you are."

"Do you expect me to believe that, Brother John?"

"I know it sounds impossible, but is not that the best reason in the world for believing? Pour yourself more wine. In wine there is truth, no?"

Before he leaves, the manuscript is safely buried in my straw mattress along with the penknife and the spare quills. I am comfortably drunk; comfortable enough to accept the blessing which Brother John murmurs over me and signs with a cross on my forehead:

"God keep you brave, Brother! God keep you brave!"

1 January 1600

Last night I slept deeply, but dreamed a carnival of confusions. I was back in Frankfurt, at the great annual fair, where I had proposed to begin a new career or at least reinvent the old one. The fair was already in progress, the halls and grounds thronged with visitors.

There was merchandise from all over the world: furs from Russia, silks from Italy, fabrics and jewellery from France, wrought iron from Germany, corals from the Mediterranean, pearls from the Orient, spices brought by Dutch traders from the Indies.

There were merchants from every country, money changers dealing in all the currencies of Europe and the Levant. There were mountains of books, old and new, and the man who strode the peaks was Wechel himself, doyen of publishers, maker of masterpieces in typography and binding who played host to all the book lovers of Europe.

It was he whom I was seeking in my dream, but always he was just around the next corner and my fear grew that I should never find him. The folk who jostled me in the crowds seemed either indifferent or hostile, or in some strange fashion, afraid of me. When I spoke to them, they turned away abruptly, and made the sign against the evil eye. The whole dream reflected the frustrations which followed my arrival in Frankfurt with my secretary, Besler.

In fact, Wechel had received me most kindly and offered me lodging in his own house while my works were being prepared for publication. However, permission for my sojourn in the city had been deferred by the Senate and I dared not risk their displeasure by taking up unauthorised residence. So I left my work in the competent hands of Wechel and withdrew to Zurich, where I still had friends and could maintain myself by private lectures.

The setback underscored the essential instability of my existence and made me all the more determined to remodel my life. Yet this very determination made me vulnerable to another illusion: that I might still be able to remedy my position with the Church and resume a normal life as a scholar-priest beyond the tyrannies of convent life.

By the time I returned to Frankfurt the admirable Wechel had procured my sojourn permit and the licence to print my works. He had arranged lodgings for me at the Carmelite convent which supported itself by offering hospitality to visitors. Also, it seemed, they reported on their guests to the Inquisition. Much later I was questioned in Venice on a report by the Prior that I occupied myself "by giving lectures to heretical scholars, and by publishing chimerical ideas and spreading novelties".

I had no means of knowing at the time that I had been denounced. It is one of the terrors of the system that one can only guess at the identity of one's accusers but never confront them to examine the quality of their evidence.

In Frankfurt I developed an agreeable acquaintance with two Venetian booksellers, Gianbattista Ciotti and Giacomo Britano. Ciotti had already established the prestigious Minerva imprint and had a long list of clients among the Venetian nobility. Among these was a certain Giovanni Mocenigo, one of the *Savi*, a Counsellor of the Republic, nephew of a former Doge.

He had read some of my works and enquired of me from

Ciotti through whom he sent me a letter inviting me to come to Venice, join his household and teach him the secrets of memory and magic. I was still considering this when a second letter was delivered by another hand. This was even more persuasive: I should be received with the honour due to a great scholar, on financial terms which could not fail to content me; I should enjoy the favour and protection of one of the most respected families in the Serenissima. Thus and thus and thus!

I had no reason to doubt the sincerity of the offer. I knew enough about Venetian politics to understand that the Republic was run by a powerful and secretive oligarchy of noble families whose names recurred constantly in the list of Doges. Even the Romans paid respect and deference to the Venetians, who they feared might one day be tempted to become Protestants in order to guarantee the independence of the Most Serene Republic. So, it was as if a golden door had opened itself before me. On the other hand, many of my friends were appalled at the risk. Italy would be, for ever, hostile territory. The Venetians were traders who would sell their own mother for a ducat! I was a fool to put my head in the lion's mouth. Obstinate as always, I paid them no heed. I rose eagerly to the lure and accepted Mocenigo's invitation to become his scholar-in-residence.

With money in my pocket and a firm promise from Mocenigo I was in no hurry to arrive. Venice in summer is a foetid city. Those who can afford it take to the hills to escape the heat and the stink. So I journeyed slowly and pleasantly through the high country of the Dolomites and arrived in Venice in August 1591. Mocenigo and his family were still away, so I stayed only a few days, then crossed the lagoons to the city of Padua where I had arranged to meet my secretary, Besler.

We had work to do, which could best be done in that city. Its university was the most famous in Europe, especially in the faculties of law and humanities. There were excellent libraries and hospitable clubs supported by a large population of foreign students, German, Hungarian, Bohemian, each with its own 'company' and national insignia. The Venetian authorities encouraged and protected them, because they brought wealth into the province and opened new opportunities for trade.

The Patriarch of Venice took another view. The presence of Protestant communities could only contribute to the spread of heresy. The Counsellors of the Most Serene Republic shrugged off the threat. They would trade with the devil himself if there were profit in the deal. They held fast to their motto: "Venetians first and Christians afterwards."

Nevertheless, under this appearance of bland accommodation, there ran a steady current of tension and unease between Rome and Venice. The Romans feared a mass defection such as had occurred in Germany and in England. The Venetians had their own misgivings. "Who goes to supper with the Pope," they said "takes a long spoon and keeps his sword-arm free."

Why is it that now, when it is far too late, I remember these things so vividly? Those days I strode like a cloud-walker, caring not at all about the difference between a Lutheran, a Calvinist, a Hussite, or a Bogomil. My concerns then were with the infinite, the spirit that informed all things. Now my vision is limited to four walls and a future about which it is idle to speculate, because I shall very soon experience it.

My first meeting with Giovanni Mocenigo was in his own palace near San Samuele. He was younger than I by about ten years, handsome and elegant in dress, married to a young woman of noble birth whom he seemed to keep constantly pregnant. He was eloquent in his welcome, though rather too eager to impress me with the breadth and depth of his learning. I was left with the impression that this was a man of moderate talent and high connections and a need to confirm both his good opinion of himself and the respect his image demanded. During our early conversations I caught a certain peremptory tone which made me as uneasy about him as he was uncertain about himself. First there was a haggle about my stipend. The amount was generous enough, but he frowned when I told him I required to be paid monthly in advance.

"Why so, Master Bruno? I prefer to pay after the service is

rendered, though I should have no objection if you drew modestly against future earnings."

"With respect, Messer Mocenigo, in the relationship to which you invite me, that of master and pupil, the service is rendered every day and all day. This is not a point I would be willing to argue."

"So be it then," he agreed reluctantly. "Now, as to domestic matters. I have children, as you know, and my wife is pregnant again, so I must ask. Are you poxed?"

"No, sir."

"Sickness of the lungs? Infectious fevers?"

"None."

"Do you drink?"

"Cheerfully, but modestly. One cannot study with a fuddled brain."

"Are you quarrelsome?"

"I do not think so. I can be urgent in debate on matters of principle, but I am not, I never have been, a brawler in taverns. I discourse mildly and keep the peace."

"Good! We Mocenigo have a name to keep."

"And I, sir, have certain civil ways to which I hold."

"Do you keep company with women?"

"When I can afford it, and the opportunity offers."

He gave me a sidelong conspiratorial smirk and challenged me.

"I know you have been a monk, Master Bruno. I know you have renounced your vows. How many women have you had?"

I gave him a shrugging, off-hand answer.

"Enough to keep me content."

"Understand then!" Once more he was the patrician condescending to a commoner. "I am tolerant of private indulgences, but I want no swollen bellies on my servant girls, no sore-tailed pages in my retinue. There are houses of appointment which accommodate all tastes in Venice. So play outside, eh!"

"I am a guest in your house, Messer Mocenigo. I respect you as I hope you will respect me."

He knew that he had gone too far and his apology was instant, if grudging.

"Please! I meant no disrespect. It is simply that, between gentlemen…"

He was at a loss for words to finish the sentence. I was happy to let him hang for a moment, twisting in the wind. Abruptly he changed the subject.

"To practical matters then. I like an ordered life, as I am sure you do. From first collation until noon, you and I study together. Afternoons and evenings are your own, but my steward must know how to recall you within an hour. There are friends I want you to meet; assemblies of gentlemen at which I may wish to present you."

"I shall hold myself at your disposal, sir."

"There is however a caution."

"Sir?"

"You will respect the confidences we shall exchange as master and pupil. You will tell no man or woman the secrets that we share. You do have secrets, yes? Disciplines of power, ancient arts?"

"I have written and lectured for years on such matters. I have taught the disciplines of memory and the arts of natural magic, both ancient and modern. But, understand me, Messer Mocenigo, the teacher is one who makes known, not one who conceals. Knowledge is like the air which all may breathe. You cannot put it in a bottle, and cork it like wine for your exclusive use."

The change in him was startling. His whole body stiffened. His eyes filmed over. He seemed to retreat inside his skin and then emerge, slowly and silently like a viper ready to strike. His voice was low and sibilant.

"So what do you offer me, the man who pays the score?"

"A lifetime's learning, sir. Little or much, it's all the wealth I own. What use you make of it is your own affair. But let me add one thought. I have come here at your invitation. To this moment I have cost you nothing. The most I can cost you is a month's stipend. Would it not be wise to make trial of each other—you of me to discover what I can teach you, I of you to test how readily you learn?"

Again he changed like a chameleon before my eyes. He laughed and clapped a comradely hand on my shoulder.

"You are bold, Master Bruno! A trifle snappish, but bold, yes. I like that! Certainly we should make fair trial of each other. Why don't we begin with a stroll through this city of mine—Bride of the Sea, Empress of the Adriatic and all the seas east to Rhodes and Askelon."

As we walked and talked I confess I warmed to him. He was full of pride in his city, its far-flung trade, the beauty of its buildings and its women, the craft of its shipbuilders who, he claimed, launched a galley every day from the slips. I noted the respect with which he was saluted on the Rialto, the cordiality of his own greetings and the formality with which he presented me: "The most learned philosopher, Doctor Filippo Giordano Bruno who, after a sojourn in the royal courts of Europe, has done me the honour of joining my household as scholar-in-residence."

I was flattered of course. Still, I could not rid myself of the memory of his extraordinary transformations. There was a deep vein of malice in him; there was also a meanness of spirit, as though life had cheated him of his just rewards. Down the long years after he betrayed me I have asked myself the question which, God knows, I should have asked myself at the beginning: "Why should one who lacks nothing in birth, money or public respect betray a man who came only to teach him wisdom?"

The full answer still eludes me: perhaps because he thought to own me and, having failed, set out to destroy me; perhaps—and this in retrospect seems the most likely—he was a dabbler, a dilettante, who aspired to eminence like his forbears, but lacked the talent or the energy to attain it.

This, I believe, is why he demanded before all else that I teach him the secrets of magical arts. He saw them as short and swift roads to power, as Midas gifts turning everything to gold. His demands were abject at first, then angry as my careful expositions failed to satisfy him.

"Look, Master Bruno! We are in my private room! We are secret here. So tell me straight. You have the Hermetic formulae? You know the Cabala? You can recite the names of power, the proper invocations? You can draw the magic squares, the pentagram? You practise alchemy? You can concoct love potions and dispel the evil eye?"

"And if I could, sir?"

"Make me an adept too!"

"To what end?"

"Why do you need to ask? You are not a stupid man. I will say it for you once, and once only. I, Giovanni Mocenigo, am bent upon high enterprise for myself and for my sons. In two centuries the Mocenigo have produced four Doges. So I have much at stake. If you can put power into my hands, you too shall have power beyond your dreaming. Be my tutor now in magic arts and you shall be my chamberlain, heart's favourite beyond the reach of Rome, the whimsical malice of any man. There now! You have my truth. Tell me yours!"

He had made himself vulnerable now. He was therefore dangerous. I answered him mildly and with all the respect I could muster.

"My lord, the things you ask I could engage to teach you. Give me vials, liquor and alembics, I could be the most proliferous alchemist in Europe. But gold from lead? No man has done it. None can. Magic? Give me chalk and compasses, a cat for my familiar, mouldy books written in gibberish, I'll make the hairs stand up on a clerk's tonsure… These are carnival tricks for knaves to practise, fools to tremble at!"

I knew he was angry with me, but he contained himself for fear that there might be other secrets I was concealing from him. I tried to mollify him by telling him of my encounter in Paris with Don Miguel Maravilloso who was both swordsmith and alchemist. He listened attentively, seeming to understand the meaning; but still he came back obstinately to the same question.

"Tell me straight, Messer Bruno, can you cast spells on people?"

"I can, sir, and so can you."

"Can I indeed? Then tell me how."

"It's easy. Walk in town. Look solemn, puffed like a pouter

pigeon. Start a rumour about any man, high or low. Premise his death, a looseness in his wife, a treachery of friends. Within a day he's cringing from the prick of ghostly daggers, fasting for fear of poison!"

He grasped this notion readily enough. His anger ebbed. His eyes lit up with malicious amusement, but he pressed the question further.

"This is what makes a magus?"

"The magus creates himself, sir. The ignorant confirm him in the role."

"How so?"

"What else is magic but play upon stretched nerves and secret fears? Love potions? Half a ducat buys enough cantharides to make a eunuch stand like a maypole, or itch the crotch of every nun from here to Vicenza. Mix it with bats' blood, or balsam, babble nonsense over it, what's the difference?"

The next instant he was on his feet, his dagger unsheathed and pricking at my throat.

"And this is the sum of your wisdom, Master Bruno! For this I pay you good gold?"

"No, sir!" I brushed away the dagger with a gesture of contempt. "This is the folly from which I wish to protect you, the folly of ignorance and superstition. You have to purge them out before you can even begin the getting of wisdom. And one more word, Messer Mocenigo: they are more quickly purged by laughter than by threats. If you want me gone, then say so. If you want me here, then pay respect to the learning I offer—a learning most hardly come by."

It was a risky moment, and I knew it. The man was a petty tyrant, more than a little mad, torn between rage and reason. I was at the same instant back in my student days in Naples, when you had to be fast on your feet to survive. Fortunately Mocenigo was a coward. He wilted quickly in the heat of a quarrel and changed just as quickly into a smiling apologetic young man. He sheathed his dagger and then offered me his hand.

"Forgive me, Master Bruno. I have much to learn from you, not least in civility. I desire you to stay and continue to instruct me."

"Very well. Do you wish to continue now?"

"No, no! Let us resume tomorrow and concentrate on the arts of memory, which are less contentious than the magical ones."

"As you please. I may take the opportunity to see some of the city."

"Good! Take a stroll over to the ghetto. It's an exotic place, and some of the Jewish women are quite ravishing beauties. You might be interested to visit the studio of our great master painter, Jacopo Robusti called Tintoretto. He is an old man now, but his sons Domenico and Marco still keep the studio active…"

He was stroking me now as if I were a cat, hoping to make me purr again. I hated it, because I knew he was beginning to hate me; yet we were tied to each other like misshapen twins in a monster birth.

From that day I began to think how I might disengage myself and cross back into Germany. I could only guess how Mocenigo might try to even the score between us, but try he would and all the subtle mechanisms of the Republic were at his disposal. Even their own Doge could not travel about without permission. They would send assassins to kill any craftsmen who betrayed the secrets of their glass-making. Anonymous denunciations were encouraged. There was a small army of paid informers. I was a foreigner here. I was also in deep trouble with the Church. I was too well known to hide easily. Any citizen on any day could denounce me with an unsigned note, slipped in the *Bocca della Verità* and any day after that the city watch could scoop me up like a shrimp in a net. Which was exactly what they did in the end, but there was a longish overture to be played before that opera began.

Mocenigo kept his promise to introduce me at various gatherings of gentlemen devoted to letters and to philosophy. They received me courteously and seemed impressed by my eloquence, the subtlety of my reasonings and by my skills in the arts of memory which it amused them to test in various ways. Ciotti the bookseller was in constant attendance because this was how he created a market for his books. There were always clerics present too, prelates of various degrees. Some of them approved me, some did not, but the civilities of the occasion were always observed. Still, I was never quite sure whether Mocenigo was using me to enhance his own reputation or compromise mine to make me more dependent upon his goodwill.

One meeting which he staged with some care, in his own house, was that with the Inquisitor General of Venice, Prior Gabrielli, a Dominican of course. His greeting was cool, and in the beginning our talk was more like an interrogation than a conversation. Gabrielli asked:

"Your name, again, just so I have it right."

"Filippo Giordano Bruno, called the Nolan."

"Ah yes! One hears the accent of the south. One hears echoes too out of old histories, matters not yet resolved, apostasy from vows, a libertine existence, suspicions of heresy…"

"These are echoes as you say, Prior; echoes and rumours and suspicions, none of them proven."

"True. But you are bold, Brother Giordano, with your case open still, to put yourself so close in reach of our enquiries."

"Prior, with great respect, I am here because I trust the justice of my cause, the charity of the Church, the noble house which gives me patronage."

"You understand you have no licence to teach publicly, nor preach in Church, nor give the sacraments."

"I do not seek it, Prior. I am, at this moment, a philosopher in residence with his patron."

Mocenigo was instant in his support.

"And I, my dear Prior, stand surety for my own guest. The Council has approved his sojourn. The Patriarch has no objections. I believe we may all profit from Master Bruno's presence in our city."

"I trust we may, my friend." Somewhat to my surprise Gabrielli relaxed and smiled. "Let me say, Brother Giordano, that I have heard you speak and found you most eloquent and persuasive. I cannot ignore the scandal of your vagabond life, neither can I conceal our concerns over the orthodoxy of your published works. However, since Messer Mocenigo here offers the protection of his name and his house, I am, for the moment, content."

"I am happy to hear it, Prior."

"Now, if you will excuse me, I need a private word with Mocenigo…"

As they walked out of the room together, I felt a sudden shiver of fear. It was, as the Germans say, as if a goose had walked over my grave. There were too many *sfumature* here, too many shades of meaning and emphasis for me to decipher in a single moment. I wore a bold front as always, but I confess I felt like Socrates as he watched the Athenians pouring hemlock into his cup.

It was early evening. My time, for what it was worth, was my own. I left a message with the steward and went out to divert myself in the city. I chose a noisy place, a common tavern near the arsenal, where sailors came and shipwrights and oarsmen from the galleys, great hulking fellows with the shoulders of oxen and giant thirsts. All the nations of the Mediterranean were there, freemen and bonded captives, Nubians and Cypriots and Corfiots and Libyans and Copts from the Nile Delta. There was a babel of tongues and a very Joseph's coat of colours and costumes. The women were of the common sort but bright and chattering as parakeets. They came begging for drinks and company and promising a fool's paradise of delights afterwards. I had learned in my wandering life to choose a companion early and entertain her in a snug comer away from the troublemakers and the predators. Most of the time the girls were happy with the arrangement. It took the weight off their feet and saved them the labour of peddling their charms to loutish drunks with shallow pockets.

I was at ease in places like this. I had been since my student days in Naples. I understood the *gergo:* the argot of life in low quarters. If someone raised a song I could sing passably well. I could strum a borrowed mandolin or embroider a traveller's tale to match those of the mariners. As I grew older, I found another quite special reward in these excursions. I did not have to debate anything. There was nothing to argue about; this was life without ornament, without pretence. These were no long-faced moralists delivering judgement because a girl was fishing in a man's pocket while he was fumbling under her skirts. There were no pat syllogisms about the nature and relationships of human kind. This was life in the primeval forest, often short, often brutal and dangerous, but always abounding with energy and sometimes touched with a special beauty, like the stinking canals of Venice calm in the dawn light, golden in the summer glow.

It was this essential continuity and fullness of experience which I had tried to express all those years ago in my dialogues, *Of Cause, Principle and Unity.*

"We are delighted by colour, not by any single colour, but a unity which contours them all. We delight in sound; not in a single note but in a harmony of many…"

Truth to tell I felt more harmony in the raucous ribaldry of a dockside tavern than in any hall of learning in Europe.

It was early when I returned from my excursion. I was still sober but with enough liquor inside me to loosen my tongue and enough successful dalliance to make me reckless. When I let myself in, I was surprised to find Mocenigo, still sitting over the supper table with two guests. One was Prior Gabrielli, the Inquisitor, the other was introduced as His Excellency the New Apostolic Nuncio to the Republic, the Most Reverend Ludovico Taverna, Bishop of Lodi. I saluted them and begged to be excused. Mocenigo insisted that I stay. He poured me a glass of wine which I sipped but did not drink. Then he led me into the talk, like a rabbit into a snare.

"Master Bruno, my guests and I would value your opinion on certain matters."

"I hesitate to offer it, sir, in such distinguished company."

"Come! You are too modest. You have travelled much, yes?"

"Too much, sir. I am very glad to be home at last."

I saw the look that passed between the Inquisitor and the Nuncio, but I took small account of it. I had just stepped out of a much simpler world. Mocenigo continued his prompting.

"Upon your journeys you have met both the high and the lowly."

"Indeed yes. I have been Lector to the King of France. I have been received by the Emperor of Prague and by the Queen of England. I have lectured in Wittenberg and Helmstedt and Oxford… But yes,

I have lived lowly too, with wandering charlatans, and horse-traders. How else does one know the human condition? How else, earn the right to talk about it?"

"So!" The Apostolic Nuncio found voice at last, a sharp emphatic voice like the crackling of twigs in a fire. "So you have sometimes kept bad company, Master Bruno."

"I have kept human company, Excellency. I have never claimed the right to judge my fellows."

"But was not that right—that duty indeed—laid upon you when you were ordained a priest, to hear confession, to give or with-hold absolution?"

"But I, sir Nuncio, declined to exercise the right because I had seen it so often abused."

Mocenigo intervened swiftly and smoothly.

"I am sure, Master Bruno, His Excellency meant no slight. We seek your judgement on a larger matter. There is, as you well know, rebellion in the air, schism and heresy and threats of new religious wars. What moves the common folk in London, Frankfurt, Wittenberg, Venice…?"

I looked from one to the other, trying to read their faces, but they were inscrutable as carnival masks. So be it then! They should have my answer, plain as I could make it.

"What moves the common folk? Boh! Hunger will cause a riot, but hand out bread and onions and it will die before sunset. Lust? That's a disturber too. I've seen a fellow cut from breast to bellybutton for a tavern trull! But when you talk rebellion, heresy, alarms of war, that's another tale altogether."

"So tell it, my friend!" This was the Inquisitor now. "We who sit upon the powder keg should like to know what lights the fuse."

"You yourself have said the magic word, Prior. Light! That's the abracadabra spell that opens the door into tomorrow. The light comes slowly but—by God!—it comes, to clown and chimney sweep and plodding serf."

"I do not understand." The Prior seemed shocked. "Is this some new and specious revelation?"

"New to them, Prior, but specious, no. No! No!" Suddenly I, myself, was on fire. I pushed myself back from the table and strode about, declaiming at them like an orator. "Look! Here on my master's bookshelves there are old maps which show the world is flat and that it ends just past the Pillars of Hercules where dragons breathing fire devour poor sailormen. There are no dragons! You know that; so do I. Westward there are the golden lands Cristoforo Colombo found, southward and east the searoads to the Indies and to far Cathay. That's light! Then there's Copernicus and after him the heavens open to an infinite universe of suns and moons and undiscovered earths."

"Seductive novelties!" said the Nuncio.

"A dangerous doctrine!" said the Prior.

"Please go on," said Mocenigo.

I was in full flight now, a bolt of lightning would not have stopped me.

"Novelties they may be, Prior. Seductive, yes, and even dangerous! But they wake men's minds to doubt and questioning. They ask who drew the dragons on the maps, cartographers or quacks? Who says the Pope sees all Creation plain, the moment after they have elected him? Who says a king rules by God-given right? There is no king in Venice. Does God dispense one right in Spain, another different here? The people ask gentlemen. Their questions make the groundswell and the tidal wave comes after."

"This is sedition!" The Nuncio was outraged.

"Hold a moment, sir!" This was yet another Mocenigo, one I had not seen before. He spoke brusquely, and with authority. Marvellously, it seemed he was speaking in my defence.

"You are a guest at my table, Excellency; Master Bruno is a member of my household. There is no sedition here. Master Bruno did but answer truthfully a question which I put to him. We may disagree with him, but not insult his probity."

"I am reproved," the Nuncio conceded stiffly. "I beg pardon for my bad manners, from you, sir, and from Master Bruno."

The Prior shook his head in disappointment. As an Inquisitor he did not make such easy concessions. I bowed to the Nuncio.

"Thank you, Excellency. I take no offence. I know well that these are contentious matters; but they do touch us all. Now, I pray your lordships will excuse me."

I walked out then, steadily enough I thought, but just slowly enough to hear a brief low-voiced exchange between the Nuncio and Mocenigo.

"That man is trouble, sir, and yet you harbour him in your house."

"You are new here, Excellency." Mocenigo was curt. "You are an emissary seeking friends. Should you not ask, first of all, the wherefore and the why of things?"

I did not hear the rest, but it confirmed what Mocenigo himself had told me: he was engaged in a game of high politics between Rome and Venice. I was simply a pawn who could be swept off the board in a single move.

From where I sit now, it all seems clear as spring water, but it was not so clear at the time. Mocenigo was a character too clever on the one side, and on the other too unsettled for me to read accurately. I had as much difficulty deciphering him as I had in my first studies of the Egyptian mysteries.

For instance, after this episode his daily studies with me became more intense and more detailed. He took copious notes and asked all sorts of questions, some subtle and searching, others irrelevant and even vulgar. He asked, for instance, how I judged the miracles of Christ, the curing of the sick, the multiplication of the loaves and fishes, the raising of Lazarus from the dead.

I answered him in the mode of academic debate. I pointed out that the Gospels were written long after the death of Jesus and that they were intended as handbooks and memorials for the use of the faithful. There were many discrepancies between the narratives. I remember making a flippant remark that since the Jews regarded pigs as unclean animals, the headlong rush of the Gadarene swine sounded more like a joke than a miracle. I also said, I remember, that Christ's treatment of Mary the Magdalene was testimony of his tolerance in sexual matters. He forgave her "because she had loved much". The Church on the other hand made mortal sin of what, after all, God Himself had contrived, and what served men and women very well and pleasantly!

Mocenigo laughed and made a note, as if it were a good joke to share with his friends. He made another when I cited my own case and claimed that the Church subverted the Gospel message when it ruled by fear and not by love.

I know now that I was a trusting fool, dictating to a traitor the terms of my own indictment. At that time, I still believed it was the duty of an honest instructor to address all questions and all opinions with his pupils. When I saw, at last, the jeopardy in which I stood, it was already too late to escape.

I told Mocenigo I needed to make a visit to Frankfurt to confer with Wechel on my publications. He refused to let me go, saying that I had not yet discharged my contract. I told him my absence would be short and as a man of honour I should most certainly fulfil my duty to him. Again he refused. This time he threatened me with forcible detention. I told him he had no right to hold me against my will. He showered more threats on me and stalked away.

That night, very late, he came to my chamber, accompanied by his manservant Bartolo and five or six boatmen from the Venetian canals. They hauled me out of bed and locked me in an office. Next morning he brought a captain of the watch with a few men who took me down to a ground-floor storeroom where they held me for a few days.

There, at three in the morning, I was formally arrested by one Captain Matteo d'Avanzo under orders for the Council of the Ten. I was taken to the prison of the Holy Inquisition to await trial on charges still unspecified.

Thus began a long agony which has consumed the last eight years of my life. Here let me add a footnote. I have never been incarcerated in comfort. Unlike certain noble captives in history I have never been allowed the support of faithful companions, of civilised discourse, or reading or writing at will.

From the beginning, everything was reduced to a barely tolerable minimum: enough food to keep me from starvation; enough warmth so that I might not freeze to death; paper and light enough only to make notes relevant to my cause. No medicine against the prison fevers; no advocate to advise me against the nameless faceless accusers who besieged me.

So, as I patch together this chronicle of the locust years, you must not blame me if I write less eloquently or less exactly than once I could. I was a prodigy in the arts of memory. Now I labour to recall details and marshal chronologies, though strangely enough, I can recall and recite dialogues like an old actor, which perhaps I am, after all.

There are moments, as after the trial of Brother John, when I am disposed to pray, but the formularies of my monastic years have become distasteful to me. So I invent my own invocations thus:

"In case you have forgotten me, Lord, I am Giordano Bruno, penny philosopher and one-time priest, magician by repute and heretic by imputation, fomentor of sedition, braggart, boozer, cloud-walker, dancing his jig upon a mountain top waiting for star fire... *Oremus,* let us pray. O God, if God there be, O Christ, if they did not kill you for ever on your Calvary, O Mother of Christ, who saw what men could do to one who heard an alien music! Bend to me. Be tender. I am a fool, a comedian whose audiences are the blind, the deaf and dumb. Or perhaps it is the other way round—I am the afflicted one and they are ashamed of my infirmity. And yet I do see visions, shout a kind of praise, feel in my pulse apocalyptic drums. The visions may be false. I do not know. The praise may be a blasphemy, I do not so intend it. The drums? You, O God, you set my heart apounding; whisper, just once: 'Be still, you are at home and safe!'"

There! I have said it and set it down: my soul's prayer, my heart's desire. But as I lay me down to rest, there is still the same question without an answer. Where is home for the vagabond Brother Giordano? And where will he fetch up at the end of his last journey?

2 January

Let me set down as a signpost the date on which I was brought from prison to face the Inquisitors of the Venetian Tribunal. It was the twenty-sixth day of May, 1592. Only a few months before, a new Pontiff, Ippolito Aldobrandini, Clement VIII had been elected to the throne of Peter. It was too early to know what, if anything, I might hope from his clemency and wisdom. For the moment the Venetians held me, locked like a bird in a cage. This prison of the Inquisition was only a short walk away from the chambers of the Chief Inquisitor and the Magistrates of the Council of the Ten. To reach them, the prisoner had to pass through the sinister interrogation room to which he would be consigned if he failed to satisfy the Inquisitors.

The first moment I stood before the tribunal I knew that I was in deep trouble: up to my armpits in quicksand and facing the heavy cavalry. The president of the tribunal was the Patriarch of Venice himself, primate of all the bishops of the Republic, His Excellency the Most Reverend Lorenzo Prioli. Next to him was the Papal Nuncio, Ludovico Taverna, whom I had met in Mocenigo's house. Prior Gabrielli I knew already as the Chief Inquisitor. Tomasso Morosini, scion of an ancient family, represented the magistracy, and with him was one Luigi Foscari, again an historic name in Venice. The assembly was completed by the Recorder, a guard and myself, shabby and stinking from my days in the cells. There was method, of course, in this humiliation. Even in the best of circumstances it was hard to maintain resolve and dignity in the face of all these grandees and the power they represented.

The Patriarch began the meeting with an invocation to the Holy Spirit, begging for light and wisdom in the deliberations. For my part I had little hope that the prayer would be answered. So many disparate interests were in conflict here. The Recorder asked me to state my name, age, parentage and place of birth. Then Prior Gabrielli, the Inquisitor, addressed me in formal terms.

"Filippo Giordano Bruno, Presbyter, Clerk Regular of the Order of Friars Preachers, you are summoned here to answer certain denunciations, touching your public works, your lectures and the opinions you have expressed in private and in public."

I decided I must join issue immediately or lose whatever small vantage place I held. I posed a simple question.

"I ask with great respect, Prior, of what am I convicted?"

"Convicted?" He seemed truly shocked. "As yet you are convicted of nothing. We are here simply to make enquiry into charges made against you."

"By whom?"

"You may not know."

"They threaten my life and yet I may not know their names? How do I challenge them?"

"We test them, sir, as we test you."

"But I am a prisoner, while they go free. Even if you prove them perjured liars I am still their victim. Is this justice?"

"It is the method of the law."

"And I have no recourse against this loaded law?"

"None, sir. We are the servants of what exists until a later wisdom changes it. The Recorder will read the charges."

"Please, there is another matter."

"State it."

"My cell is damp, my food a bite above starvation. I am racked with rheumatic pains. Since I am not yet a criminal, may I have the courtesy of a chair?"

There was a sudden chill in the room. It was as if I had uttered an obscenity. They all looked towards the Patriarch. He waved an impatient hand at the guard.

"Bring the man a chair! He cannot stand all day like a stork while we reason his case. Now, may we get on with our business?"

A chair was brought. I sat down. It was a small victory, but it gave me courage. The Recorder picked up his papers and began to read the bill of indictment.

"The Nolan is accused first of holding opinions contrary to our holy faith, of having discoursed against the faith and its ministers. He holds erroneous opinions on the Trinity, the Divinity of Christ and the Incarnation. He holds erroneous opinions on Christ himself, on the holy Mass and on transubstantiation. He claims that the universe is infinite and eternal. He believes in the transmigration of souls even from humans to animals. He does not believe in the Virginity of Mary, the Mother of Jesus. He practises the arts of divination and of magic. He has indulged in the sins of the flesh. He has lived among heretics and adopted their doctrines and manners. These are the general heads of the document; the particulars are even more scandalous. The Nolan has stated, for instance, that the miracles of Christ were conjuring tricks; that priests and friars are asses selling them to other asses; that the Church corrupts the message of the Gospel and seeks to convert by fear and not by love; that man must use his own liberty to come to God."

He paused to draw breath. I could not hold back a contemptuous comment.

"My lords, this is a very long catalogue."

"Of most vicious error," said the Nuncio.

"Too many for one man, Excellency!"

Morosini, the assessor for the magistrates, offered his own curt comment:

"This document lacks sobriety. It is clearly written in haste and anger."

"Thank you, my lord." I was grateful for his intervention. "And may I add that this denunciation contradicts itself. First, it claims that I am a heretic who rejects the sum and substance of the faith, while in the same breath I plead an apostolic love, a need to come to God in liberty. What does he want, this nameless enemy? To toss a coin and have it come down head and tail at once?"

The Patriarch leaned forward and spoke directly to me.

"Are we to understand that you deny each and every statement in the charges?"

It was a tempting lure, but I did not rise to it. I needed to lay a broader base for my defence. I told him: "No, Eminence. I deny the import and conclusion of the whole. I claim a malice in the informant, a malversation of my words."

"Can you explain this, please?"

"Look, sir! Four of us here are clerics, schoolmen trained in argument and disputation. The others are jurists familiar with the logic of the law. You know how we were taught, by pro and contra. One day we stand in the debate and say 'There is no God! Refute me!' Another day we claim the opposite. It is the method, honourable and approved from Aristotle to Aquinas. Does that make us heretics? Surely not! But any fool or knave hearing our talk could wrench it out of frame and burn us for it."

The Patriarch nodded agreement and gave a direction to the Recorder:

"Note that the accused does not deny the formal words imputed to him. He does deny the taint of heresy and claims a malice in the informant."

Once again Morosini added his own note in support:

"As assessor for the Republic, I request a new interrogation of the said informant."

"It shall be done," said Prior Gabrielli, then turned back to me. "Now, Brother Giordano, not without reason, you object to anonymous testimony. We understand the objection though we cannot admit it. Let us stand, therefore, upon more open evidence: the record of your life and the books which bear your name upon the title page. Can you agree that?"

"Most willingly, Prior. But on condition that I may still interpret my own words and myself."

"Should they need interpretation?" This was Taverna, the Nuncio, hostile and contemptuous.

"Always, Excellency! Always! A simple example: you are out walking on the Rio del Palazzo. You feel a sudden call of nature. You lift your robe and you expose—saving your reverence—a pubic part. A passing maid cries, 'Gross indecency!' You claim a simple need: piss or burst. The act still needs explaining!"

They all laughed, and for one brief moment I thought I had them on my side. The moment passed all too quickly and the interrogation began again.

If any who may read this memorial should ask why I, in my present extremity, should rehearse these old dramas, let me explain that they are still as vivid in my mind as on the day they occurred. This was my first pitched battle with the Thrones, Dominations and Principalities of the Church and the secular State.

Never before and never afterwards was the course so clear, the enemy so plain in view, the hope of victory and vindication so bold. Given what I had at stake, given the odds against me, there was a certain epic challenge. Once, in Paris, at the fencing school, I had seen Miguel Maravilloso, the master, take on three swordsmen at once and disarm them all in two minutes. My bout would be much longer, but on that long ago day I did believe I could win it.

The Prior walked me steadily through his brief.

"…begin with the open book of your life: you are now forty-two years old. You were schooled in Naples. You studied Logic, and Philosophy and Humanities."

"I did. I had good teachers too—Theofilo da Vairano, Vincenzo Colle il Sarnese. I remember them with much affection."

"At seventeen, you became a novice in the priory of San Domenico. In the current records you are described thus: 'an avid student, with a prodigious memory, a captious tongue, a will not easily bent to discipline'."

I could not resist a small joke at my own expense.

"Hold our youth against us, Prior, and most of us would be gallows meat!"

That raised a small laugh and the Prior hardly faltered in his recitation.

"You took vows then. You promised solemnly to live in poverty in chastity and obedient subjection to the Rule of the Order. Yes?"

"I did."

"You were ordained a priest."

"I was."

"And then you broke your vows. You fled the convent and the priesthood. Yes or no?"

"Yes."

He paused then, to let the tribunal digest my admissions. The next question came from Tomasso Morosini, assessor for the magistrates. He asked in the mildest fashion: "Why did you do it, Master Bruno?"

"Why? This is old history, my lord. Let me try to reconstruct it for you. I take it you have never been a monk?"

"Never! Thank God, the Church and I have both been spared the experience."

"So let me describe it. A monastery, my lord, is a very little world, shut in behind stone walls. There are few saints—very few! There are some who live in simple goodness. There are others who, inside the Church or out, would sell their sisters for a pastry cake. I was first accused of an impiety. I refused to wear medallions of the saints clustered like Bacchus' grapes around my neck. I still preferred the symbols of our founder: the rosary and the crucifix."

"But these too you later abandoned?"

"Please, my lord, let me finish first. Another time—and this was when it became serious for me—I found a brother monk fumbling in my papers, sniffing for heresy like a pig for truffles. I was reading and making notes at that period on the world of Master Erasmus of Rot-

terdam. His books were forbidden to be read except with permission.
I hid my volumes in a privy, where they were later discovered.

"Immediately guilt was presumed: I was arraigned for trial by
the Master General in Rome. I knew what that meant. We Friars
Preachers are ourselves Inquisitors. I had no answer then—nor have
I now—to malice and conspiracy. So, I fled."

Out of the brief silence that followed my admission, came the
dry voice of Taverna, the Nuncio.

"The scripture has a word to say on that, does it not? 'The guilty
fleeth when no man pursueth.'"

I was choked with anger and I rounded on him.

"Do not judge me, sir, by tags and texts! True justice is dispensed
far otherwise!"

"You are insolent, Master Bruno!"

"Am I, sir Nuncio? Sit here and feel the sword blade on your
neck. Let me pelt you with scraps of holy writ. See how you like
it!"

The Patriarch intervened firmly to stifle the quarrel.

"We must control ourselves! This is a tribunal and not a bear
pit. You must admit, Master Bruno, this flight of yours does bear a
colour of guilt."

"I know it, Eminence. I have never denied it."

"Had you then the wit to face down your accusers and to trust
the loving kindness of our Mother the Church, you might not now
stand in such jeopardy."

"Eminence, at twenty-five, a rebel and afraid, our Mother
Church seemed like a giantess, neglectful of her brood, heedless of
all their miseries."

"She was and is your mother."

"And I, her son, still find her breasts are dry, her hands much
less than gentle! Please, Eminence, may I stand and stretch my aching limbs?"

"Be free. We are not gaolers but judicial inquirers, seeking a
common truth."

I was only halfway to standing when Taverna sprang his trap.

"And, Brother Bruno, this would be one truth! You went to Zurich and became a Calvinist: a renegade, a chaser after false and alien needs."

"No, sir!" At least now, I was on my feet and facing him. "I was a troubled soul, trying to find a hat to fit his bursting brainbox!"

"And you found it?"

"No! This restless imp who rides upon my back, forbade me such a peace. I quarrelled with those Swiss sobersides and spent a little time in gaol."

Taverna had made his point. Like any good duellist, he pressed hard to hold the advantage.

"It would seem, Brother, that you are neither fish nor fowl. Among the heretics you are the orthodox. With the faithful, you are more an unbeliever than Julian the Apostate!"

He was waiting for my response. I knew there was no profit for me in this line of argument. I tried another. I asked him, "Excellency, have you ever had a son?"

"How dare you impute—!"

"I impute nothing, Excellency. It is a fact of life in our time that some clerics, even many senior ones, have offspring whom they acknowledge in various forms, and maintain out of their ecclesiastical benefices. I accept without question that you have no son. Neither have I. But, if we had, would we not watch him grope his way from infancy to manhood, testing himself against this strange new world? Would we not pity him and stretch a father's hand to lift him up from darkness into light?"

"If we love, we try. But, when he comes to manhood, do we hold him safe from all his follies?"

"I use your own words, Excellency: if we love, we try. So, I put it to you and to all these gentlemen. The Church is our common mother. How do you see me, sirs? A son, a brother or an enemy?"

He was back, swift as a striking viper.

"We do not know. That is our problem! A heretic can have no part in Christ, nor in the assembly of his saints. We note, you see, in all your wanderings, in England, Germany and France, this curious circumstance. Your friends are mostly of the rebel breed: Lutherans, Huguenots, Calvinists, Hussites and Waldensians. Your lectures and your disputations—such as have been delated to us—all seem to reject the classic lines of Christian argument. You must not blame us if sometimes we smell a wolf under the sheepskin!"

The Patriarch raised a moderating hand. "In spite of that, we wish to treat with you in charity."

"All of you? You, Prior? You, Messer Morosini? You, Excellency?"

It was Morosini who answered with cool irony. "A word to the wise, Brother Bruno! Do not bet your life on our Christianity. Convince us!"

"In God's name, how?"

"Be patient." The Prior was beside me now, notes in hand. "Answer the questions as they are put to you. Be assured that in the end we shall arrive at a common ground of truth. Now, be seated, Brother, and let us continue."

In this new mood of sweet reason, he was more dangerous than before. His first question was deceptively simple.

"So, Brother Giordano, we are agreed your books are you. No argument?"

"No argument, except—"

Taverna slapped hard on the table-top. "Always exceptions! Never a plain answer!"

Morosini smiled and shrugged. "The man is a philosopher! He needs a definition of the terms."

"Let us define then." Gabrielli was too calm for my comfort. "What do you need to know, Brother, before we proceed?"

"Prior, like me, you are Dominican?"

"Yes."

"We learned the same theology?"

"Yes."

"Our masters said free speculation is allowed on every matter but the substance of the faith. Do you agree?"

"I do."

"So, when I reason in my books on nature and the natural order, whether I am right or wrong, I am beyond attainder, yes?"

"Yes. But, if you make one step beyond the natural into the realm of faith, you fall under the law."

"Whose law, Prior? Before I piously consent to kill myself according to your codex, may we please examine it together?"

"My God!" Taverna was on his feet, now protesting vigorously to the Patriarch. "The man's a legal trickster, spinning a web of courtroom sophistries just to distract us!"

"Am I, sir Nuncio?" I forced myself painfully to my feet, so that I might confront him eye to eye. "Let me show you what I am! One man, without a single advocate or friend in court. I have not slept too well because of rats and damp within my cell. I have not prepared my case. You, only you, have seen the documents. Besides, there is no candle in my cell to read by. I face you, five judges, a clerk and an armed guard. Behind you, what? The majesty of Venice and her Empire, the might of Rome and all the princes who support her, all the army of the orthodox. I pray you, then, give me at least the time to argue for my life! Or finish this base comedy and burn me now!"

There was a long silence in the room. No one was ready to answer the challenge I had laid down. Finally, the Patriarch rose in his place and delivered his decision.

"Brother Bruno's point is well made. I urge upon my colleagues to refrain from harassing the accused and to respect his right of argument. Please proceed, Prior."

Gabrielli referred to his notes and then addressed himself to me.

"You asked for a statement of the law. We put it thus: our Saviour, Jesus Christ, came down to earth, God in human flesh, and gave us all a revelation of eternal truth. He left, to Peter and his successors, the keys of heaven, authority to preach, interpret and unfold the moral code implicit in the truth. That is the right of Peter, held by the reigning Pontiff. The rest of us, bishops and priests, may use the right by lawful delegation only. Are you answered, Brother?"

"No, Prior! Your answer begs the whole question of apostolic continuity and papal power. This is the rock upon which Christian Europe has wrecked itself. We have had a council, Trent. Its decrees cut Europe like a cheese. Thenceforth, we were perforce Catholics and non-believers. Europe at the core is Christian. How long can such a perilous division last? The answer hangs upon a subtler question yet, Prior: what are the limits of power? Put in philosophic terms: how absolute is absolute, whether of maximum or minimum? Who says with certainty what is a matter of faith and what of proper speculation?"

I must give the man his due respect. I had put him in a dilemma but he did not shrink from the horns. He stood his ground and gave me a carefully measured answer.

"The limits are defined, from time to time, by papal documents, the councils and the Church's common word."

"But the limits change, Prior! So, what may burn me now, tomorrow may make me saint and doctor of the Church. You see my problem! At his last supper with his disciples, Christ blessed bread and wine and shared them at the table. He said: 'Take this, eat it. This is my body. This is my blood.' It was an act of mystery. He did not explain it. In the Christian family, that act is repeated and shared with joy and hope. Now, we have stuck a name on it, like an apothecary's label: transubstantiation. Christ himself had never used the word, nor heard of it. Paul would have choked on it! I am accused—anonymously—of magical practices. What kind of magic have we here? Natural magic? Mathematic magic? Necromancy? Help me, Prior! Help the dispensation of justice in this place."

"I cannot, Brother, because the question is not relevant. You asked a statement of the law. You have it. I will not argue us into absurdity."

He was clever and practised. He was clear of the horns now. He had sidestepped them and was already in another arena. I had no choice but to follow him. He picked up two volumes from the table and showed them to me and to the tribunal.

"These are two of your titles: *Of Infinite Worlds* and *Of Cause, Principle and Unity*. You did write them?"

"I did, yes."

"A curious thing: the inscriptions on the flyleaves say 'Printed in Venice'. Were they not, in fact, printed in England?"

"They were."

I tried not to show how shocked I was. They had delved deeper than I had discovered.

"So, you and your publisher have connived in a lie?"

"If you put it so, yes."

"What other way should I put it?"

"You might perhaps note, with a certain tolerance, that this was a commercial stratagem, common enough and counselled by my publishers."

"For better profit?"

"Obviously."

"Does not this make you a venal man?"

"It denotes a poor one, Prior. Scholarship is no high road to riches."

"It also marks the man a liar!" said Taverna.

"A petty falsehood." Morosini discounted the charge. "None of us, I think, would want him hanged for it."

"Of course not!" Taverna did not press the point. "It should, however, make us cautious about his credibility."

It was clear that this sorry little revelation had lost me much ground. I wondered where the Inquisitor would lead me next. He held up the volume, *Of Infinite Worlds*.

"In this work, you state that the universe extends beyond our vision to infinity. Our world is only one of many. Do I have it right?"

"Yes, you do."

"Then, are we not, at one single stride, into heresy? Is not infinity an attribute of God and only God?"

"There is no contradiction here. You will note that I say that the infinite Creator is coextensive with his infinite Creation."

"You say more!" He turned to a marked passage. "You say:

'*What we call the Creator is that spirit which animates us all.*' Already you are out of nature and into faith. You are in conflict."

"I did not mean it thus."

"But thus you wrote it. Your books, you said, are you."

Another foothold was lost to me. I needed to gather my wits and regroup my arguments, but the Inquisitor gave me no respite. He handed me the book and commanded me: "Please read the passage I have marked."

Normally, I am fluent, even an eloquent reader. This time, I was dry mouthed and stumbling. Even to me, the author, the text sounded hollow as a gourd.

"*The soul, the anima, being a thrust of eternal energy continues after one body's death, to animate another, be it human or animal…*"

I closed the book and handed it back to the Prior. He laid it deliberately on the table, then gathered himself in silence while the others, silent too, waited for his summation.

"Brother Bruno, in this book of yours we have two propositions; both are, at face value, heretical. The Church has always taught that God, an eternal and infinite being, is infinitely greater than His own Creation, that while He sustains it, He still remains separate. Next, the Church has always taught that human souls do not migrate to other bodies. So it would seem that at least two of the charges brought against you are well founded."

This was the moment Taverna had been waiting for: a formal imputation of heresy from my own works. He leaned back in his chair, sardonic and dismissive, as if the whole case against me was already made.

"I think we'll find, gentlemen, as we walk Brother Bruno down the road, that the denunciation made against him is a true bill of particulars, written by an honest man, as shocked as we are by the opinions of this self-styled philosopher. What say you, Brother? Better confess it now than stretch the patience and credibility of this tribunal."

Now I was backed against a wall. I needed all my wit and strength to make a lunge at my adversary.

"I will not confess, sir Nuncio! I stand on my first claim—freedom to enquire, hold and express opinions on any subject in the natural order. I further claim that everything I have written or said conforms in substance to the Deposit of Faith. Give me paper, pens and ink, give me my books, a copy of the bill against me, time and some light within my cell and I will prove my orthodoxy, point by point. Errors there may be, but of expression, not intent. These I will happily recant and edit out of all future printings."

"Now there's a serpentine concession." Taverna was relentless. "'I am absolutely right,' he says, 'but if I'm wrong, I'll change it overnight.' This fellow will keep us here a twelve-month with his sleight of hand. Give him paper enough, he'll scribble us all into the grave!"

"He has a right to answer, does he not?" For the first time, we heard from Foscari, the Inquisitor, who had sat silent through the proceedings to this point. He looked old and ailing and his voice was weak, but to me, he sounded like the Angel Gabriel announcing the possibility of salvation. "We have the duty to hear his answers and he has the obligation to recant when convinced of error. He offers that. Why not accept?"

"Because I do not trust him. He shifts and changes like a weather cock. He is a liar, self-confessed!"

"In spite of that"—Foscari was a very persistent man—"we have a clear commission: sober study, a dispassionate verdict, a sentence fit for what misdeeds are proved."

To which the Patriarch added a saving grace note. "We must also have a merciful concern for the immortal soul of this, our troubled brother. I propose we adjourn this session to a time convenient for all. We have agreed to take further depositions from our informant. Let that be done. The Recorder will reconvene us. The guard may remove the prisoner. My thanks to you all, gentlemen."

As he was leading me back to my cell, the guard, a decent country fellow from the marsh country near Roverna, told me cheerfully: "That was a close call, little brother! The way things were going I thought they'd have you on the rack before sunset. That Nuncio fellow is a nasty one! Watch out for him next time."

Looking back at him now, across the chasm of the years, I see Taverna not so much as an enemy, but as a prototype of all that I have found repugnant in conventual life and in the Church itself. As a bishop, he had been vested with pastoral office for the care of souls. In his hands, however, the crozier had changed to a sword. The pastor had become an agent of the body politic, contemptuous of the people from whom he had been separated too long and too far.

I had asked him a clear question. What was I to him: son, brother or enemy? He had declined an answer, inventing instead another category: the heretic, who had no part in Christ or his family. Politically, the definition served very well. There was no hope of cure. The diseased member must be surgically removed. All argument about the treatment was futile, even dangerous. The disease could spread and destroy the whole body.

Every panel of Inquisitors which I faced over the next seven years contained at least one, and sometimes more, replicas of Taverna: pragmatic, peremptory, pitiless, and deeply divided within themselves. They would open their arms to the repentant Magdalen, their hearts to the returning prodigal, but to the puzzled questioner, the pilgrim on a darkening road, crying for light, they were adamant.

The problem, the mystery, is that they are always there; they always have been, they always will be, to the world's end. Amen! These excursions into memory are proving more painful than I expected. Excuse me, my lords. Ladies, I can do nothing but dream of you now. Goodnight.

3 January

This morning, when he makes his morning rounds, my gaoler, the surly one, tells me I am listed for a bath and some barbering before the Master General visits me three days hence on Epiphany.

Thinking to make a joke, I beg that this time the water in my tub be hot. He curses me roundly. What right have I to complain about anything? Soon, I shall be grateful for even a drop of cold water. They'll be roasting me like a hog on a spit and I'll be burning for ever in hell afterwards.

The sheer grossness of the fellow shocks me deeply. I cannot even raise an anger against him. Yet, when I lay out my paper and begin sharpening a quill, my hands are unsteady and my mind is in tumult.

To calm myself, I begin a little private game which I learned at school in Naples. On a sheet of my precious paper, I make a series of small erotic sketches: men and women in various positions of sexual congress. They represent memories of my youthful escapades as *postiglione per le puttane* and my late visits as a client to various houses of appointment in Europe.

I have a small skill in drawing and a large one in visual memory, so the drawings flow vigorously from my quill.

The memories come flooding back, and with them the pricklings of a lust which I had thought to be dead in ashes long ago. I begin thinking that the drawings would work well as illustrations for *The Lascivious Sonnets* of Pietro Aretino.

They called him the scourge of princes because of his skills as a satirist and—so rumour said—as a blackmailer. I never met him. I was only seven years old when he was born and much older when I came upon his writings. As I work at my bawdy little cartoon, I think how much I would have enjoyed his company.

Halfway through the morning, the black fog lifts from me. I lay aside my sketches, folding them into the mattress with the completed page of my manuscript. Then I settle down to write again. Instantly I am back in Venice, facing the tribunal of the Most Holy Inquisition.

They were collecting all the evidence and all the witnesses they could lay hands on, and confronting me with it in a series of intense interrogations. Their tactics had changed, too. They were no longer walking me steadily through a prepared brief; they were harrying me on every side, seeking to corner me, like hounds in pursuit of a fox. The Prior read me a passage from a deposition:

"The Nolan said these things: 'Christ was a sad fellow, who seduced the people with his magic tricks. He feared death and tried to flee it.' Do you remember the words, Brother?"

"I could perhaps, Prior, if you prompted me as to the informant who reported the words, and the occasion on which I am alleged to have uttered them."

"You know we cannot do that."

"So, you ask me to respond to an allegation from a nameless individual about a conversation on an unspecified occasion. Come now, Prior! This is too much! I cannot answer."

"Cannot or will not?" This from Taverna, alert and snappish as always.

"Should not!" Morosini was still apparently my defender. He

turned to the Patriarch. "Eminence, we have all read the testimony upon which this question is based. To some of us, it is highly suspect. We must not expect Master Bruno to hand us a sword to kill him with!"

"I agree." The Patriarch belonged to the city as much as to the Church.

The Recorder asked a careful question. "How shall I record this, Eminence?"

The Patriarch reflected a moment.

"The accused claimed that without further information, which the tribunal was not disposed to give him, he could not answer the question. Our colleague, the Apostolic Nuncio, imputed this as a refusal. Messer Morosini took the opposite view, with which I concur. Now, please, may we pass on."

Respites like this were rare. I was tiring under the pressure, and at day's end I was consigned to the damp horror of a prison cell in Venice and the company of other unfortunates who would sell me out for an extra spoonful of polenta. I was not afraid of them. I should have been because, in sheer defiance, I became reckless in my speech with them.

Prior Gabrielli raised one question which showed how widely the nets had been spread.

"I read you a text. You wrote it in your book, *Of Cause, Principle and Unity.* You speak of this Elizabeth of England who usurped the throne, murdered the rightful heir and blasphemously calls herself Head of the Church, Protector of the Faith. This is what you say: *I praise her, the divine Elizabeth, a queen in title and in dignity, whose presence sheds bright light on all the world, whom no prince can excel in knowledge, art or generosity.* The words are yours?"

"They are."

"The lady is a heretic, a persecutor of the Church."

"Let me say that I have not been in a position to question her on doctrine, and that she has never persecuted me, although I was known to her as a Catholic. I do not ask this tribunal to condone what I have written, only to consider in mitigation certain facts: I was much at court—the Queen's court. I was guest of the Ambassador of France, a Catholic gentleman, most loyal to the faith. He did not—and I hope you will not—make a courtly compliment a test of orthodoxy. As to the epithet 'divine', this is the fashion of speech in a woman's court. A brooch, a ring, or a ribbon are all 'divine'! The Queen herself can hardly merit less."

There was a small chuckle around the room. The Patriarch moved swiftly to stifle it with a reproof. "Good Brother, it would seem you were more courtier than Christian."

"I was, sir, and I regret it."

"I'm sure you do." Taverna was snapping at my flanks again. "You know—none better—that in the early Church the test of faith was to refuse to name the Emperor Divine."

"It was not made a text in London. Besides, my faith was known and never abdicated."

"What was your faith, Brother, when in prison here? You declared to a fellow prisoner: 'Christ our Lord committed a mortal sin by setting himself against the will of his Father. In the garden he prayed "Father let this chalice pass from me".' Did you say that?"

"I said more. He reported less. In so doing, he lied."

"Can you explain that, Brother?"

"Easily. What I said was: 'It might seem that Christ committed a mortal sin… It might seem that he refused to do the will of his Father', and I added: 'So in the end, he bowed to his Father's will.'"

"Why should we believe your version?"

"Why should you believe the other, unless you are already decided to convict me out of hand!"

"Did you deny that hell exists as a place of punishment, eternal punishment?"

"I expressed doubts on the manner in which this is taught. I find it hard, I confess I still find it hard, to understand why the Creator would waste His infinite power to create a charnel house. But I remind Your Excellency that honest doubt is by no means heresy. Were you not taught that in theology?"

"Did you not say that Moses was a clever magician, skilled in the magic arts by which he vanquished the magicians of Pharaoh?"

"Please! Please! Please!" Morosini was on his feet, appealing to the Patriarch. "Eminence, may we not have some common sense here? I hold no brief for the accused, God knows, but it shames me to see him petted with charges like a peasant in the stocks!"

The Patriarch was clearly perturbed. He did not want to make an enemy of the Roman emissary. He waited a long moment before delivering a hesitant rejoinder.

"Perhaps, Messer Morosini, you would like to explain your objection more fully. You must understand that charges have been laid and they must be answered."

"With great respect, Eminence, I do understand that; but let me explain myself with a parable."

"You have our leave. Provided the parable is not too long."

"It is very short. You know, every Venetian knows, the little lane, a step or two from San Marco. They call it the Street of Dolls, where they make carnival masks and children's puppets."

"I trust there is a relevance here." Taverna was not happy.

"Patience, sir!" Morosini was smiling now. I, myself, was intrigued by this parable. "To make a puppet, they begin with a wooden manikin—no face, no eyes, just limbs and trunk and head. They are all alike. Then the puppet maker begins to paint. A few strokes and there's a harlequin. Mouth up, he's laughing. Mouth down, he's sad. A change of clothes, a hank of hair, then he's a she, a lady of the finest quality. You see our Bruno sitting there. You've heard him argue. He is beyond doubt an intelligent man, a scholar of repute. But this other Bruno—the Bruno of rumour, anonymous report, malicious malversation which we in this tribunal have confirmed for ourselves—this other Bruno is a figment, a jumping doll, beyond reality. No living man can match him—be he saint or satanist, as much a heretic as Arius, as great a saint as our own Anthony of Padua! This ends my parable, sirs!"

He had done better by me than I could have dared to hope,

though I could not begin to understand why. He had subdued the tribunal to silence. I sat in the middle of it as in a dark pool, with the water up to my neck. Taverna, the Nuncio, rose in his place. He was calm and surprisingly restrained. He smiled and raised his hands in a gesture of surrender.

"Let me say first with great deference that Messer Morosini has done us all a service. There is confusion here. There is contradiction. We have not perhaps dealt with it as skilfully as we might. So, we must take swift action to mend matters."

"What action does Your Excellency suggest?" The Patriarch was eager for a solution.

"Put Bruno to the Question!"

It took a moment for the shock to register. I was the last to grasp the horror of it. Taverna was demanding that I be submitted to torture to elicit a confession. I felt suddenly dizzy and nauseous. I buried my face in my hands. The guard grasped my shoulders and hauled me upright.

The Prior was protesting: "No! I will not consent! The intention of the law is clear. The court shall not put any man to torture who has not displayed obduracy and contempt."

"And I say, Prior, that on the evidence of his performance here, Giordano Bruno is a liar, contemptuous of us all."

"I disagree," said the taciturn Foscari. "He has not refused to answer, therefore he is not contumacious. The only lie we have proved against him so far is the attribution of his books to a Venetian publisher and on that he admitted the truth to us."

"I note the disagreement." The Nuncio was implacable. "The Recorder should note it, too, then note what I am about to say. As Papal Nuncio to the Most Serene Republic, I represent the Head of the Universal Church, His Holiness Pope Clement. With this, my patent in the name of God, I demand that Giordano Bruno shall immediately be put to the Question. Now, gentlemen, what do you say?"

It was Morosini who answered first.

"A small reminder, Excellency."

"And what is that?"

"The instruments of death and torture are at the disposal of the Republic and not the Church. Not here in Venice, sir!"

Taverna flushed in sudden anger.

"Do you refuse me, then?"

"Not yet. I wait upon a formal and polite request from Rome, through you, to the Republic, which in this court is myself."

I remember most vividly that strange suspended moment in which I was more intent upon the skill of the two duellists than upon my own fate which hung upon the outcome. Taverna, the diplomat, replied with cool formality.

"Messer Morosini, I request, formally and with profound respect, cooperation to complete the work of this Most Holy Inquisition."

Morosini took his time. He could afford the luxury. My time was running out. I heard him sign me over like a basket of fish in the market.

"To aid the faith and further to cement the friendship of Rome and Venice, I consent."

I must have fainted then. I remember nothing until I woke to find myself being dragged by two guards back to my cell, and tossed inside like a sack of corn.

Next morning, they handed me over to the torturers for my first experience of pain. They stretched me on the rack until I could swear they had separated every joint in my body. I will not dwell on it here. Tales of human torment are a commonplace, and for me there is much worse to come before my day of liberation from this sick world.

Let me record simply that when I woke in my cell, agonised by cramp, trembling with fever, Morosini was standing over me, stirring me with his foot. I heard him mocking me, but I could not see his face in the gloom.

"Poor little man! So puffed up with your fine philosophies. You cannot even read the weather signs! The thunder's rolling round your ears, and you are still listening for nightingales! Wake up, Master Bruno. Wake up!"

I tried to turn, but every movement was torment. I asked, "Who are you?"

"A friend." He held up the lantern so that I could see his face.

"God save me from such friends!"

"He cannot. He is a prisoner like you of theologians and Inquisitors. I am the only one who can help you now."

"You! You sold me to the torturers!"

"Not sold. Just lent." He was mocking me again. "To teach you, friend, a necessary wisdom."

"Give me water, for the love of God. I am burning up."

There was a wooden pail of water. With a ladle, close at hand, Morosini scooped up water and held it to my lips. I drank greedily and fell back, exhausted by the effort.

Morosini asked, "Can you hear me and understand?"

"I understand, my lord. Only the believing's difficult."

"I like you, Bruno." God! He was so bland, so coldly and contemptuously bland. "You are much a man; but no man is ever enough to beat the last turn of the rack, the last hoist of the pulley."

"Go away!"

"Do you know who denounced you?"

"Mocenigo."

"More, my friend. We have depositions and letters and verbal innuendo from all and sundry. Brother Celestine the Capuchin, Graziano the Neapolitan, other prison friends with whom you've joked and cocked a snook at piety. There are volumes of petty treacheries, enough to burn a dozen Brunos!"

I told him I was sick of his sick world. He laughed and shrugged.

"They will not let you out of it so easily. They will tread you, Brother, like grapes in a vat. They'll tan your hide and hang it on a wall and say, 'Look! This was another heresiarch, another Arius, another Luther!'"

"Heresiarch! My God. How do they dream these fantasies?"

"They do not dream, my friend. They are the most pragmatical of men, as I am."

"What do you want?"

"To cheat the Mocenigo, spit in his shifty eyes. Do you know yet, my little Socrates, why Mocenigo betrayed you?"

"He wanted me to teach him magic. I could not, would not stoop to mumbo jumbo. He thought I cheated him."

"O God! The innocence of scholars! Look! You were a gift from heaven for Mocenigo. He wants the Doge's cap, which he will never get. He seeks the support of Rome. He thinks to buy it with you, a bright new heretic."

"But you?"

"I want you to confess, tomorrow. Not to guilt, at least not too much guilt! Only to error and to ignorance. Sign whatever abjuration they dictate."

"And then what happens?"

"Then you belong to Venice, not to Rome. We sentence you. A modest term of penance in a pleasant convent where the wine is good and the books are plentiful. When you're forgotten in a year or two, we'll give you gold, safe conduct and a horse, and send you packing back to Germany."

"I wish I could believe the half of it."

"Unless I can convince you, you are lost. There will be more of this rough medicine until they break you—body and mind."

"Give me a grain of hope."

"It's simple, isn't it? Let them burn every page you ever wrote; you can write again, so long as you are alive! Dead, they will scatter your ashes to the wind. And who will hear the wailing of your ghost at midnight? Listen, little man. I tell you simple truth. We are all beleaguered here. Rome is vowed to stamp out heresy. Venice is pledged to be the Most Serene Republic until the dawn of doomsday. I want you free to thwart this scheming Nuncio of ours and put the evil eye on Mocenigo. Where do we end? We play with tarot cards. Whoever gets the Hanging Man is marked for death. We pity him but let him die, because we are all forest beasts who want to live. Well, Brother Bruno?"

"More water, for the love of God."

He poured more water down my throat and then took a small pewter flask from his breast pocket and unstopped it. In a mad moment, I thought it might be poison, but he gave that crooked ironic smile and reassured me.

"Don't worry! It's a draught to make you sleep. My apothecary prepared it. You can dream on what I have proposed. If you agree, then I'll have you cleaned up and made comfortable before you face the tribunal and make your recantation."

A strange, irrelevant question passed my lips. It was as if another man were speaking my tangled thoughts.

"Why, Messer Morosini? Why have you robbed me of my anger?"

"To give you back your life, Brother Bruno."

"I wonder if I really want it. I wonder..."

I did want it, of course. In that place, after my first taste of prolonged torture, I wanted it desperately. As the opiate began to take effect, I felt relief and euphoria and trust enough to commit to the bargain Morosini had proposed to me: no admission of specific guilt, but a general abjuration of errors into which I might have fallen, an expression of penitence for my personal misdeeds.

Yes, I told Morosini, I could wear that much sackcloth, even with a few extra ashes sprinkled on my head. He told me, at least I think he told me, he would see to the rest of it. I did not hear him go. I did not hear the slamming of my cell door. I was mercifully adrift in a wasteland, on the far, far edge of time.

One more act of this drama still had to be played out. Some days later, still shaky and limping but clean and barbered, I was brought again before the Inquisitors. They were, I think, a little shocked by my appearance, but it was clear that Morosini had prepared them for my act of abjuration.

Prior Gabrielli was gentle with me this time. He asked: "Giordano Bruno, are you an honest man?"

I confess I smiled at the question. It seemed an odd way to begin. I answered with what humour I could command.

"Yes, Prior, by and large I am. Sometimes more by and sometimes larger. Still, I think at core I'm honest."

"So, I ask you, having a care for your sick body and your troubled soul, will you recant your errors?"

I was restored enough by now to be cautious. These men were great dividers and subdividers, splitters of legal hair. I framed my answer with deliberate care.

"In general, Prior, and truthfully, I can admit to errors in writing and in speech. But pin me to particulars—without a text, without the strength for argument, I could admit monstrosities. I will not do that."

"Would you in a penitential time—and penance would be imposed, but clemency extended—would you in sober quiet examine all your texts, confer, reflect and finally recant whatever particulars might be shown false to apostolic doctrine?"

"Yes, I would promise that—reserving still the scholar's right of argument."

"Which, given the scholar's goodwill, none of us here would deny. Are you, Excellencies, all in agreement?"

I heard no words, only a rustle like a small wind blowing over the table. The Patriarch raised his hand in summons.

"Approach the table, Brother."

As I stood up, my legs buckled under me. The guard lifted me up, led me to the table and forced me, not ungently, to kneel. I had to support myself by leaning on the table edge.

The Patriarch spoke again. "There is no formulary. Address yourself as if to God."

I closed my eyes, and prayed to an absent God to send me the words. They came slowly and painfully.

"My lord, I have, with all sincerity, searched heart and conscience. I know that I have given cause for scandal by my personal life and raised suspicion of heretical tendencies in my writings and speeches. I am ready to reform my life, repair the scandal, reject the heresies I have entertained and the erroneous opinions which, if they are contrary to faith, I most heartily abhor.

"For my sins and errors, I ask a humble pardon of my God and of you, my brethren and superiors. I willingly accept the punishment you will determine for me and I beg… I beg…"

It was then that words failed me. I collapsed, crouching on the floor, my face buried in my hands, sobbing uncontrollably. The guard helped me to my feet and led me back to my chair. I was still sobbing when Taverna, the Nuncio, stood to challenge the assembly.

"That was a moving scene, a hopeful sign of regeneration, perhaps. But Rome will not be satisfied. There are charges still outstanding there and in Naples against this man. Therefore, I must serve notice on the Church of Venice and on the Republic that the Holy Office requests the extradition of Brother Giordano Bruno to face further trial in Rome."

I was shocked out of my weeping into a state of frozen terror. Morosini was instantly on his feet, protesting.

"You cannot do this, sir Nuncio! This court had already closed its case."

"I do nothing, sir!" This was Taverna's moment of victory. "I am servant and messenger of His Holiness, as you, sir, well serve this Most Serene Republic. We should not quarrel. Let our masters fight the battle, eh? They'll come to terms. Now, if His Eminence will give me leave, I bid you all good day."

It was a day of black despair. Betrayed once more, I was bereft of hope. I had no will to fight. I lacked the energy even for speech. When they took me back to prison, I was a shambling mute. I had to be supported on the shoulder of my guards to reach the cell. When they offered me food, I gagged at the sight of it. All I could hold down was water. When I tried to sleep, I was knotted with cramps, trembling with feverish signs. When I slept, fitfully, I was haunted by nightmares of mocking demons. I screamed for help, but no sound issued from my lips and no help came, either.

Yet, strangely enough, my prison condition did improve. I was moved to a higher and drier cell, with a small barred window through which I could see a patch of sky, and to which there came each day a pair of pigeons, who rested and preened themselves on the ledge. A few days after the move, I was summoned to the presence of the prison Governor. He had both a message and counsel for me.

"There are certain noble gentlemen who much regret the turn things have taken for you. They regret that certain promises made to you have not been kept. They are working to prevent your extradition to Rome, or at least to defer it as long as possible. They have asked me to make certain improvements in your conditions here. As you will have noted, I have already begun to change things for you."

"I have noted it, sir, and I am grateful."

"Then take my advice. Choose your prison company with care. Do instantly what the guards order. And bridle your tongue. By all report, you have in the past been too garrulous for your own good."

After this, my spirits began to lift. It was not only the better conditions, but the fact that I had now a clear respite from interrogation and the constant threat of torture. To all intents and purposes, the Venetians had finished with me. My encounter with the Romans was at least being deferred, and my health was beginning to improve. I took the Governor's advice and sought out the prisoners least likely to compromise me.

One of these was a *nostròmo*, a boatswain from one of the big galleys which traded along the Dalmatian coast and as far east as Cyprus. He had got drunk one night and made an affray with the watch, during which he had uttered some blasphemy, to the effect that the Muslims administered better justice than so-called Christians. The affray earned him a fine, and the blasphemy an uncomfortable encounter with the Inquisition. I told him I had problems of my own with the Holy Office and that we should both stay a long sea-mile from that subject. After that, we became friends and he kept me entertained for hours with tales of his travelling life.

He had the practical man's clear perception of political reality. The Adriatic belonged to the Venetians, who did not believe in free trade. From Venice, they controlled the north; from their fortress in Corfu, they controlled the southern entrance to the Adriatic gulf.

They demanded, and violently enforced, that all merchandise entering or leaving the Adriatic must touch Venice first. No merchant vessel could sail for Crete, Corfu or the cities of Dalmatia without paying a levy that guaranteed the arrival of their goods first on the docks of Venice. Infractions were swiftly punished. The saltworks of Trieste were demolished. Venetian galleys harried the grain ships which supplied the merchant republic of Ragusa, which was, at the same time, a vassal of the Turks and protected by the Papacy.

But, as my sailor friend informed me, the system was "a net full of holes". Goods were smuggled all the time on the rivers and overland routes of Dalmatia and through the smaller ports where the great ships of Venice could not enter. Iron from Trieste was sold in Italy, wool and wine went from Apulia to Kador, and the corsair raiders took their toll from it all. He himself had to swim for his life when a galley on which he was serving was attacked by twelve Turkish galliots just off Valora.

On the other hand, he had earned enough to buy himself two women, sisters from the slave market in Trieste, who, even as he spoke, were waiting at home to welcome him—waiting and working, of course, keeping the beds warm and the money box full until he was out of this scrape. His post was still open to him. Good seamen were hard to find and the merchants who owned his ship had already made a petition for his early release.

When I asked him what sort of work his women did, he grinned and said:

"What women do best, of course, but they work from my house, not the streets. My friends from the galleys are their best customers, and they keep away the troublemakers. I have to pay tribute to the watch, of course. Nothing is left untaxed in the Serenissima, but the system worked well enough for me until I opened my big mouth and said that Islam was an easier religion to handle than Christianity. Don't you agree with me?"

I had been warned off this ground, so I simply smiled and murmured a banality: *i gusti son gusti*, each man to his own taste. That, too, could easily be translated as heresy, but I could have said much more: that you don't teach a man to love God by stretching him on the rack, and you don't justify the rack by telling the victim that Christ, too, suffered scourging and crucifixion. Why do I recall this faraway moment in what will certainly be my final deposition? For one thing, it gave me the same pleasure as I enjoyed in my youth, sitting under an oak tree, swapping stories with a classmate. For another, it helped to rid my mind of the clutter I had accumulated over the years: the elaborate mythologies, the creaking literary conventions, the vocabularies of theologians and philosophers.

I am so tired of all this! If God speaks to us at all, it must be in our mother tongue. How many of us know another? If He shows Himself at all, it is in the wonders of every day, the flash of bird wing, the opening of a blossom, the face of a sleeping babe. It is not too hard to believe in resurrection when, out of the 'little death' of the act of love, a child is born, and when the same child is nourished by the grain that grows out of the mouths of the forgotten dead.

For the rest, what is it? Boh! Garbled patter, meaningless gestures to distract the audience and make them believe the tricks of the conjurors. This is one of the counts on which they will kill me. I claimed, they say, that the miracles of Christ were conjuring tricks. In fact, I said something quite different: "Jesus had no need of conjuring tricks. He, himself, was the message and the miracle. Those who recorded his life felt the need to embellish it with wonders. They were mistaken."

What does it matter now? When I am dead, the lie will become a legend to justify injustice. The babble will go on. The mountebanks will make their magic in the squares on market day. The real miracle will continue every day, unmarked, except by the few who have the grace to see it, and the many who, like myself, see it, prize it, but all too soon must absent themselves from the joy of it. A bedtime thought. Tomorrow, I am to be barbered and bathed. There will be no time to write, with a coming and going of people, the risk of discovery will be too great. I pray that the bathwater will be hot.

4 January

My bath and the visit of my barber have both been deferred until tomorrow, the eve of Epiphany. This is what they do to you in prison: tease you with small hopes, then, when you reach out to grasp them, snatch them away. It is one more petty cruelty to remind the dancing bear that his master holds the rope which delivers the pain. There is no recourse from it, except to feign indifference, which for this tease is not too difficult. I know they will have to clean me up before the visit of the Master General and I have a day free to continue this chronicle.

In the last months of my prison sojourn in Venice, I had no clear idea of what was going on outside. I knew that the Romans had claimed me and that the Venetians were resisting the demand as an affront to their sovereignty. I was simply the *volano*, the shuttlecock in their game of statecraft. Pope Clement VIII, Ippolito Aldobrandini, had been nearly a year on the throne, but he was an obstinate and formidable negotiator, better cultivated as a friend than turned into an enemy.

So, by a majority vote of the Senate in January 1593, the Venetians decided to surrender me to the Holy Office in Rome. I was put on a ship which carried me to the Adriatic port of Ancona. Thence, I was transported by road across the Apennines.

I left the prison in shackles, but on board ship the shackles were removed, and when we travelled overland to Rome, I was still free of them. A winter journey across the Apennines was long and rough. We spent much time hauling and pushing our heavy vehicle out of bogs and snowdrifts. My guards were companionable enough. We shared shelter and food and wine and gossip at the inns along the way. But once we came to Rome, I was shackled again and delivered to the Governor of the prison of the Holy Inquisition.

He gave me a frosty welcome and read me the rules decreed by the Holy Office for the conduct of detainees: no conversation, day or night, between cells nothing to be read or written which did not have direct relation to one's trial. No exchange of messages or letter; deprivation of both medicine and legal aid; and, if a prisoner proved uncooperative, punishment, specifically by torture, could be inflicted at the discretion of the Governor for any breach of discipline. It could also be inflicted by sentence of the tribunal if the prisoner refused to answer with complete openness all questions put to him, even those which might reveal new faults or inculpate others. Every month, the tribunal would be presented with a list of the prisoners and the progress of the cases against them.

After that welcoming oration, I was hustled off to a dark and gloomy cell somewhere in the bowels of the building. Over the years, I came to learn that this building had once been the palace of a certain Cardinal Pucci, that it lay close to Saint Peter's and right next door to the barracks of the light cavalry. The upper front were the offices of the Inquisition itself. The lower ones, the stables and cellars, subterranean storerooms, were converted into cells. So far as we prisoners were concerned, we might have been cave dwellers on the moon. My first cell, I know, was below the level of the Tiber and the damp ran down the walls.

However, being an incurable optimist—incurable fantasist, more like!—I told myself that I was now living in the Pope's own domain and that, sooner or later, I would be able to make my appeal directly to him. This, I believed, was my right, *de facto* and *de jure*. If all other justice failed, where else should I turn but to the successor of Peter, vested by Christ with the plenitude of power: to bind, to loose, to make and unmake things, to gather up lost souls from the highways and byways, and bring them to salvation.

I knew, of course, that before I could reach the Pontiff, I should have to be ground once more between the millstones of the Inquisition. The Roman process would be longer than the Venetian one. There would be much more to cover, many more depositions to be taken. Nonetheless, I believed that, if I could hold out long enough against the tribunal and stay out of the hands of the torturers, I would stand one day in the presence of the Vicar of Christ and receive both his absolution from censure and his personal affirmation of my orthodoxy.

Now my dream has turned to Dead Sea fruit—dust and ashes in my mouth. My appeals have reached the Pope. He has refused to read them. One small vestige remains, like the last autumn leaf fluttering in the winter wind.

On Epiphany day, which celebrates the coming of the Magi to visit the infant Jesus, the Master General of my Order will come to visit me in private. His position in my regard is an equivocal one. I have fled the jurisdiction of the Order, but I am still subject to it. I have asked many times to be released from my vows, so that I may re-enter the familial life of the Church as a simple priest. Such a release has to be granted judicially by the Holy Father, but normally it would be granted without question on the insistence of the Master General. He has refused to press my petition. He still claims me as a member of the Order. Therefore, prodigal though I be, I am still a son of the house. I have claims on the charity of the family as well as in natural justice.

The Master General is a highly intelligent man. He knows this argument as well as I do, but he is caught in yet another snare. The old and great religious Orders like the Friars Preachers and the Franciscans, are, in effect, the legions of the Pontiff. They are mobile, they can be sent anywhere in the world. They are responsible directly to the Holy See and not to local bishops. They are the shock troops of an imperial Church and, while they are respected, they are also feared by provincial authorities, whose power they limit or curtail.

The leaders of these religious Orders, the commanders of the legions, are therefore men of power; but their power, too, is limited because they are elected by ballot of the members of the Order for a limited term, and they are pledged, in any case, to obedience to the Holy See. In the case of the Friars Preachers, their remit has for centuries included the control of the Inquisition.

So, my problem defines itself simply. If the Master General will intercede for me with the Pope, I have a chance. If he does not, then I am lost.

You see how important is this simple matter of bath and barbering. I do not want to present myself to my spiritual father like some waif from a wayside ditch. I need his respect more than his pity. I want him to commend me to His Holiness as a scholar of substance, open to wise counsel and correction. I do not want to be dismissed with contempt into a dubious eternity.

It is not without significance that in all the ceremonies of excommunication, the word 'degrade' is repeated several times and a cleric of high rank is appointed and paid a fee of two scudi to perform the act of degradation.

I can write no more today. The contemplation of my sorry state has reduced me to so deep a melancholy that I contemplate opening my wrist like Petronius Arbiter and lapsing quietly into oblivion. Unlike Petronius, however, I shall have neither the sound of music nor the gentle talk of friends. I still have time to choose a better moment—besides, who knows to what nightmares I might wake.

Epilogue

Bruno was now fifty-two. Although his body had been tortured and weakened by the long and painful years of imprisonment, he remained obstinate in his resolve. He knew in his heart that he had not turned his back on God; he still believed that what he disputed was not in opposition to God, but merely questioned some of the assumptions. His repeated requests to be given the opportunity to explain his beliefs and philosophies were constantly met with denial. Bruno's frustration increased when he was denied the chance to articulate his views before the papal Inquisitors.

On 20 January 1600, Bruno was once more brought before the Inquisitors, this time in the presence of Pope Clement VIII. All his previous petitions to the Pope had failed: Clement had simply refused to read or consider them. There is no doubt that the Pope ordered the trial be completed and sentence pronounced. Bruno had been betrayed before by promise of liberty if he recanted, and so finally accepted the futility of his search for truth. He realised that the Inquisition and the Church were threatened by his questions and observations, and that no man would be prepared to consider his explanations. The reality and brutality of his choice was clear. He refused to recant. He chose to take the option of dissent, which cost him his life. Heresy was punishable by death by burning at the stake.

On 9 February, the Notary of the Inquisition, Flaminio Adriano, read aloud Bruno's sentence to him and the gathered assembly. After mentioning the main events in Bruno's life, and listing the eight heretical propositions, the sentence was read as follows:

> Having invoked the name of our Lord Jesus Christ, and of his most Glorious Mother Mary ever Virgin, in the cause of the aforesaid causes brought before this Holy Office between, on the one hand, the Procurator Fiscal of the said Holy Office, and on the other hand, yourself, the aforesaid Giordano Bruno, the accused, examined, brought to trial and found guilty, impenitent, obstinate and pertinacious; in this, our sentence, determined by the counsel and opinion of our advisers, the Reverend Fathers, Masters in Sacred Theology and Doctors in both laws, we hereby, in these documents, publish, announce, pronounce, sentence, and declare you, Brother Giordano Bruno, to be an impenitent heretic, and therefore to have incurred all the ecclesiastical censures and pains of the Holy Canon, the laws and constitutions, both general and particular, imposed on such confessed impenitent, pertinacious and obstinate heretics, wherefore as such we verbally degrade you and declare that you must be degraded.
>
> And we hereby ordain and command that you shall be actually degraded from all your ecclesiastical orders, both major and minor, in which you have been ordained, according to the Sacred Canon Law; and that you must be driven forth, and we do drive you forth from our ecclesiastical forum and from our Holy and Immaculate Church of whose mercy you have become unworthy.
>
> And we ordain and command that you must be deliv-

ered to the Secular Court, that you may be punished with the punishment deserved, though we earnestly pray that it will mitigate the rigour of the laws concerning the pains of your person, that you may not be in danger of death, or of mutilation of your members.

Furthermore, we condemn, we reprobate and we prohibit all your aforesaid and your other books and writings as heretical and erroneous, containing many heresies and errors. We ordain that all of them which have come, or may in future come, into the hands of the Holy Office shall be publicly destroyed and burned upon the Square of Saint Peter, before the steps, and that they shall be placed on the Index of Forbidden Books.

And as we have commanded, so shall it be done.

And thus we say, pronounce, sentence, declare, degrade, command and ordain, we chase forth and deliver, and we pray in this, and in every other better method and form, that we reasonably can and should.

Thus pronounce we, the Cardinal General Inquisitors, whose names subscribe this document.

Bruno listened to the sentence, faced the Inquisitors and responded: "At this moment, gentlemen, perhaps your fear in passing judgement on me is greater than mine in receiving it."

On that day he was degraded, handed over to the Governor of Rome and incarcerated in the Tor di Nona, one of the senatorial prisons on the left bank of the Tiber, not far from Ponte Sisto and Mole Adriane. It was the prison which housed the most dangerous criminals of Rome.

It is interesting to note that one of the men who signed the document of Bruno's condemnation was Cardinal Robert Bellarmino, known to his contemporaries as the meekest of men, and yet he took part in the trials of both Bruno and Galileo. Bellarmino was canonised in 1930.

Bruno was given a further eight days in which to recant, but he remained stubborn in his resolve. On 17 February 1600, a delegation of monks and priests of Sant'Orsola went at six a.m. to the Tor di Nona. Again they requested that Bruno recant; again he refused. Bruno was then undressed to the waist, covered with another garment painted with flames, and taken to his place of death in the Campo dei Fiori. There he was undressed and, naked, tied to a pole and burned alive. The accompanying monks sang litanies throughout.

There are contradictory reports of Bruno's final moments. Some report that he was gagged to prevent him uttering more heresies. According to one passer-by, Bruno was purported to have said that he was dying as a martyr and willingly, and that with all that smoke his soul would certainly have gone to heaven. According to another, he was "cursing and did not want to listen to anyone". Kaspar Shoppe from Breslau, a contemporary of Bruno, who was present at his sentencing and death, records the death scene thus: "When the picture of Christ was presented to him, he pulled back and refused it with an angry look."

Bruno might well have unwittingly penned his own epitaph in one of his Latin works, *De monade*, published in Frankfurt in June 1590. His writings were often characterised by mythological imagery and the use of pseudonyms. The rooster appears as a character in *De monade*, and Bruno put the following words into its mouth:

> I fought a lot; I thought I could win, but fate and nature repressed my studies and my efforts. But it is already something to be on the battlefield because to win depends very much on fortune. But I did as much as I could and I do not think anyone of the future generation will deny it. I was not afraid of death, I never gave in to anyone, I chose a courageous death instead of a coward's life.

*   *   *

On 9 June 1889, on the spot in the Campo dei Fiori where Bruno died, representatives of the faculty and students of the University of

Rome unveiled a statue of Bruno executed by the sculptor, Ettore Ferrari. A medal was struck to commemorate the event; its inscription reads: *To Giordano Bruno, from the century he guessed at, in Rome, on the place where he was burned.*

Bibliography

The research for this novel was prepared from the following works:

Aquilecchia, Giovanni. *Giordano Bruno* (Istituto della Enciclopedia Italiana, Rome, 1971).

Bossy, John. *Giordano Bruno and the Embassy Affair* (Yale University Press, New Haven and London, 1991).

Bruno, Giordano. *Cause, Principle and Unity* (translation and introduction by Jack Lindsay; International Publishers, New York, 1962).

Bruno, Giordano. *The Expulsion of the Triumphant Beast* (translated and edited by Arthur D. Imerti; Rutgers, New Jersey, 1964).

Ciliberto, Michele. *Giordano Bruno* (Editori Laterza, Rome, 1990).

Encyclopaedia Britannica (William Benton, Publisher, 1968).

Firpo, Luigi. *Il processo di Giordano Bruno* (Salerno Editrice, Rome, c. 1993).

Galli, Gallo. *La vita e il pensiero di Giordano Bruno* (Marzorati Editori, Milan 1973).

Horowitz, I.L. *The Renaissance Philosophy of Giordano Bruno* (Coleman-Ross Co. Inc., New York, 1952).

Mercati, Angelo. *Il sommario del processo di Giordano Bruno con appendice di documenti sull* (Biblioteca apostolica vaticana, Vatican City, 1942).

Nappi, Andrea G. *Giordano Bruno, quattro tempi drammatici* (Guida Editori, Naples, 1982).

Nelson, John Charles. *The Renaissance Theory of Love* (Columbia University Press, New York, 1958).

Singer, Dorothea Waley. *Giordano Bruno: His Life and Thoughts* (Henry Schuman Inc., New York, 1950.)

Spampanato, Vincenzo. *Vita Di Giordano Bruno* (Messina Casa Editrice Giuseppe Principato, 1921).

Yates, F.A. *Giordano Bruno and the Hermetic Tradition* (Routledge & Kegan Paul, London, 1964).

Thanks to Patrizia Vismara for assisting with some of the Italian translation.

About the author

Morris West

Morris West was born in St Kilda, Melbourne in 1916. He graduated from the University of Melbourne in 1937 and took up work as a teacher in New South Wales and Tasmania. During this period he had been a member of the Christian Brothers but left the order after 12 years. During World War II he worked as a cipher clerk in Darwin and for a time was private secretary to W.M. Hughes.

Around the time of the publication of his first novel in 1945 he worked in Melbourne radio but left after two years to manage Australian Radio Productions. In 1955 West left Australia to further his career as a writer. During his time away from Australia he lived in Austria, Italy, England and the USA. He returned to Australia in 1980.

West wrote over thirty novels, many plays and several of his novels were adapted for film. He died while working at his desk on 9th October 1999.

The fonts used in this book are from the Garamond family